# CITIZEN
# SURVIVOR
# TALES

# CITIZEN
# SURVIVOR
# TALES

# BY RICHARD DENHAM

EST. 2019

BLKDOG

www.blkdogpublishing.com

## Other titles by Richard Denham

*Citizen Survivor's Handbook*

*The Britannia Trilogy*

*World of Britannia: Historical Companion to the Britannia Trilogy*

*Weird War Two*

*Weirder War Two*

*Arthur: Shadow of a God*

*Robin Hood: English Outlaw*

Maryanne Coleman was a popular journalist who worked for The Ministry during the 1940s. While under the guise of a reporter for *The Southern Herald*, her role was to interview a variety of survivors of 'The Great Tribulation' which had plunged Britain into chaos.

She travelled throughout Britain speaking to a wide assortment of characters and those who had come to the attention of The Ministry and to collate information, both overtly and covertly, on the current state of the nation.

Although her interviews were later recovered, Maryanne herself went missing. Her fate is currently unknown. It must be conjectured that one of the interviewees was involved in her disappearance.

Here then, is a collection of thirteen of Maryanne's most interesting, amusing, bizarre, frightful and compelling interviews.

Dear Sirs,

The following accounts you are about to read were collated throughout the 1940s by the journalist Maryanne Coleman who at the time of writing was in the employment of the Ministry of Survivors. Coleman was part of a department known as the 'community cohesion unit', their role being to gauge levels of morale and resolve among individuals and communities in the aftermath of the Great Tribulation both overtly and covertly.

We have collated ten of her most interesting interviews with a varied selection of Citizen Survivors throughout Britain for the purposes of posterity, reference and future data analytics. Coleman's introductions and comments as printed in the news at the time are included (redacted as required to meet the current security needs) to provide as full a picture of the time as is thought necessary. Redactions are not shown – anyone with full clearance can apply to this office to see the originals, though it is only fair to say that permission is unlikely to be granted.

Please note, these accounts are *not* for public dissemination and to distribute them, knowingly or unknowingly, to anyone below silver clearance will be considered an act of treason.

The fate of Coleman is unknown but if she is still alive she must be considered an enemy of His Majesty and reported to the relevant authorities *immediately*. Failure to do so will also be considered an act of treason.

Please view case file 43/5453/GBS for her information and last known whereabouts.

Yours faithfully,

Agent Steed - 2565

# THE VETERAN

Richard Denham

**Name: William Sponge**
**Location: Nottingham**
**Occupation: Unemployed (veteran)**
**Threat level: 3**
**Article clearance: Silver**
**Case file: 57/4356/GBR**

**William Sponge is well known to many readers of these pages as a survivor of the Battle of Brighton. He was blinded during that battle and was also severely injured. He now sleeps rough at Thoresby Colliery, where a community of unwaged veterans and others has developed. He is luckier than many as he is eligible for charitable donations from the WVS and the John Bull Co-operative Society. Interviewing Mr. Sponge is never easy, as his memory is sometimes just a thought unreliable – however, many people choose to be generous in their assessment of the veracity of his claims and he is probably one of the richer denizens of the Colliery community. I met him in a nearby pub; as this paper does not give fees for interviews, he insisted on a drink before he would speak to me; however, once he gets going he is difficult to stop, as the interview below may show.**

**How did you end up stationed at Brighton?**

I won't lie, when I was told that my unit was going to be stationed at Brighton I was absolutely delighted. On most days, it felt more like a holiday than a posting. I visited Brighton when I was a boy once with my family in the summer, so this really was about as lucky as it got.

The evacuation of Dunkirk had happened two years earlier; I was there, and it seems like a lifetime ago. I was injured during the evacuation, nothing brave I'm afraid, no fighting the SS hand to hand, I simply slipped as I was climbing a rope onto a trawler and managed to do in my leg, leaving me with a permanent limp. The war had never really started for the BEF (British Expeditionary Force) and our evacuation was treated as a victory, which I suppose in some ways it was.

After the horrors of Dunkirk, the main bulk of the BEF pulled back to Crawley. Due to my injury, I spent a bit of time at Cambridge military hospital in Aldershot and was then posted to Brighton about four months later. A lot of my unit had injuries or other conditions that meant the brass thought they were not physically fit, but as our job was manning static defences such as pill-boxes and bunkers and patrolling the beach-front it didn't really matter. It would be unfair to think of the lads as 'lesser soldiers'. It takes a lot of discipline to be vigilant and man a post day in day out in a lovely seaside town where two years have passed. My favourite posting was on a Vickers machine gun with another lad in sandbag defences along the sea front. Not only did I have company and someone to chat with but we'd often get talking to the locals who'd fill us up with tea and cakes. The smiles we got from some of the ladies too made it all worthwhile.

It's fair to say it wasn't a complete jolly. The beach had been closed off and littered with landmines and wrapped in barbed wire soon after Dunkirk. 'Brighton Rock' was our name for the defences that to us were unbeatable. Tens of thousands of people were evacuated as Brighton was an obvious target for any invasion by Jerry.

**Was there much fighting in the build up to 1942?**

Aerial bombardments did happen, however, the formations, the Dornier bombers, Messerschmitt's and Focke-Wulf fighters, which the lads had some brilliant nicknames for, came from across the channel usually passed straight overhead towards London or wherever they were going. The deafening drone of a squad of fighter planes is unforgettable, but, in a morbid way, there was something almost exciting about it, that the action was happening elsewhere, to other people.

There was one time that will always stick with me, it was during the afternoon and people were going about their business walking up and down the promenade. A few dozen German planes flew over, people had almost become oblivious to it as we were rarely the target but we were the target that day. The Germans dropped their bombs, I didn't see the damage I was in a fortified base at the time, which was actually a requisitioned hotel overlooking the sea and the bombs fell behind us but I sure as hell heard them.

The planes though, rather than going back across the sea, made several runs, it must have only been five minutes but it felt like a life-time. They fired their machine guns down the promenade, and my God, did I see that! You can't even put it into words, to see people who were a few moments earlier chatting, being torn apart by machine gun fire. Although death is death, there is something indiscriminate about a bomb which is hard to explain, but for these civilians to be targeted made my blood run cold. When the fighting had stopped and the noise had died as the planes left, there was an awful silence in the town, a silence of only a few seconds, but I'll always remember it. Then the noise of the dying and injured sounded out, there must have been a hundred bodies that I saw littered along the promenade. My unit was assigned to assist with getting the injured to safety and disposing of the bodies, it was the worst night of my life. After that, the drone of fighter planes stopped being exciting and became the inescapable sound of dread and terror.

**How did that raid affect things?**

Things became a lot more solemn and serious after that. Where before the brass turned a blind eye to a few things, they were now breathing down the back of our necks every day. My unit was to keep a constant lookout and make hourly reports to our officer's post, which was a mile or so inland. We were trained constantly on how critical our task was; if the Wehrmacht got a foothold on the coast, they would then be able to pour in from there and threaten all of England. I must be honest though, me and the lads went through the motions, but the idea of them actually invading was unimaginable. We had been bombed by planes on and off, but that was it. Maybe our posting, two years without firing a shot in anger or Brighton itself had made us soft, I don't know. What on earth would Jerry want with Brighton, we'd say, it has no real strategic importance, no real industry, no threat. If there is fighting, surely it'll be in Portsmouth or Southampton.

Hindsight is a wonderful thing they say. There was a point where Jerry was flying more and more planes, always past us, but there was a week of very intense attacks inland. I remember our Captain speaking to us – you could always tell when he was worried because he would chain-smoke – he told us to be on our guard and prepare for an attack by sea any day. I think that is something that sticks with me, me and the lads didn't know and weren't told anything, and I wonder how much the brass actually knew as well, but questions like that are beyond my pay grade.

**What happened the night before the attack?**

I was in a fortified hotel along the seafront, there was me and another, Jonesy, on a Vickers machine gun. There were other lads scattered throughout the building and all along the sea-front. Some of them had elephant guns and artillery and mortars were all behind us inland, so we felt ready for whatever was coming. The order had been given for civilians to evacuate the town a few days before, but most people seemed to ignore it, and there was only so much we could do if they were that adamant on staying. I will remember that night overlooking and overhearing soldiers ordering civilians off the beach-front, most of them going peacefully, some being forced into the back of vans. Lots of planes were flying overhead that evening, and there was just enough light to make out the shape through Jonesy's binocs, they were four-engined, so possibly bombers or even parachutists. It turned out to be the latter, because at about one in the morning when I was eating from my mess tin, the Sergeant burst in on our room, which had been a guest room, and told us that the Germans had in fact landed men further inland and beyond our positions but we were to stay put, as there were reports of the Kriegsmarine gathering across the Channel.

The next few hours were the longest of my life, I was nervous, shaking, my mouth was dry and it sounds funny, but I wanted *something* to happen, just to break the long wait, that was the worst part, waiting for something you didn't know was going to happen or not. As the sun began to rise Brighton beach slowly came to light with its barbed-wire, hedgehogs and sandbags and beyond that as the fog cleared, one, two, ten, then hundreds. The whole sea seemed to be lit up with a grey wall, these were German ships and they were coming our way.

There is a saying in the army that all plans fall apart as soon as the first shot is fired, and that is completely true. Planes were flying back and forth overhead, some ours, most theirs, but we were oblivious to that, believe it or not. It was the ships we were focussed on, and then the bombardment started.

You see the flashes on the horizon from the warships, and the noise, the noise of the shells approaching you in the air, like a gas blowtorch, you could actually see them fly above us, exploding a hundred yards or so behind us. Each salvo seemed to get nearer to us. The noise, it's something you can never explain, it's not just a noise, it shakes you, the building, your bones. It was maddening, a few shells hit our hotel, the shockwaves punched the air out of our lungs.

There was no let up, no chance to regain your thoughts, no time to see what was happening in front of us, it was relentless. The internal walls between the guest rooms had been smashed through by my unit so we could get to each other quicker, it was a very surreal sight, being able to see three or four rooms along in either direction. A few of the men were obviously screaming their hearts out, not that you've have had a chance of hearing it. Most of us remained calm, or at least gave the impression we were. Jonesy was shaking, and I noticed I was too. I remember one of the lads of the ground floor couldn't take it, I saw him run out of the front door down the sea front and, I do not exaggerate, he was torn apart by hot shrapnel, his torso ended up thirty feet from his legs, there was steam coming off both parts of him. Horrible stuff.

The seafront curves slightly, and I was able to see one of the hotels nearly half a mile down the line take a direct hit, despite the sandbags and other defences, the whole front of the building came off, like a lid on a tin on sardines, and ten men must have fallen out to their deaths too. It was only then I realised how pathetic our defences were, other men were in bunkers, we didn't have a chance.

Then there was a silence, it seemed like an eternity but it must have been just a minute or so. It gave us long enough to gather ourselves and prepare our weapons and return the sandbags to the window that had been knocked off by the shockwaves. At that point I think it hit us, where was the RAF, the Royal Navy? Were we really the first line of defence against this unstoppable wall of battleships? The whole sea was now alive with landing craft, as far as the eye could see in both directions. Men were shouting orders, but they were muffled and incomprehensible, our eardrums hadn't recovered. It's moments like that when you realise how lonely a battle is.

Our artillery and heavy guns began to fire from inland, but it seemed pathetic compared to what was coming at us, whether many of them had been damaged in the salvo I don't know but it seemed to me at that time they were like peashooters, falling harmlessly into the sea. As one of the landing craft approached, though, it did take a hit, and ended up in a way that it floated rear first into the sea, I could make out the figures of men still alive, sliding downwards, trying to clamber over those who were dead, as they all sank to the sea. I could tell by their helmets they were Germans, if it needed to be confirmed at all.

I remember my Sergeant grabbing me by the shoulders 'Get ready! Don't shoot until the bastards are in the water'. And with that, one, then two, then dozens of landing craft began pulling up, and men climbed out into the water, wading pathetically it seemed at walking pace at chest or neck height. Jonesy took the ammo belt and that's when I began to open fire.

**This was the first time in the War you shot in anger? How did it make you feel?**

It sounds odd, but I think you detach yourself from it, you have to. The whole thing seemed very clinical when I think back, I would strafe left and right, watching the first row of men in the water collapse into the sea, they were in no position to fire back and at this point I almost felt sorry for them. Particularly the few who just stopped in the water at head height, perhaps hoping I wouldn't notice them. As groups of them made it onto the beach, I began to be more selective in my fire, firing in short bursts to conserve ammunition. I think Jonesy wasn't doing well, I remember him screaming at the top of his lungs in his thick Welsh accent for more ammunition, but no one appeared able or willing to help him. The Germans started hiding behind the hedgehog defences, but these devices are too thin to offer any real protection, and I was able to strike limbs easily.

I remember one sad sight of a German soldier, a medic I think, who simply rose to his feet and threw his white helmet to the ground in frustration as the man he was attending was littered with bullets. I did not fire on him, but someone else did a few moments later, his chest burst in a hail of bullets.

Our sea-front defences gave it a good go with what we had, the odd landing craft was sinking after being shot from further in land and the odd plane was crashing due to FLAK fire or our fighters but it was just a numbers game really, for every soldier I'd take down, two more would appear somewhere else and there were simply too many. As some of them started advancing up the shingles, the odd soldier would be blasted into the air, twisting in bizarre circles as they hit a mine. It was only when the first German soldier managed to sprint to the ground wall of our building and out of my sight did I first fear for the worst.

They must have lobbed some grenades into the ground floor as there was a violent rumble, and plaster from the ceiling sprinkled down on us. I could actually hear the odd bullet whistling past my room and smashing into the wall beyond, and the sound of bullets hitting our gun. Jonesy stood up in a panic and told us we had to go, a bullet pierced straight through his neck and he collapsed to the floor, twisted in a way that his back must have been broken by it, he didn't die straight away, which was the hardest thing. I wish I had put a bullet through his head to ease his pain, but at the time, I could only think of crawling out of the room on my stomach. I ran down the stairs to the ground floor with my rifle; it was chaos, I don't know what was happening at the front of the hotel as I ran out of the rear exit with a group of other lads, barging past the dead and dying. I remember just sprinting, the weight in my lungs, bullets whistling, the man next to me being pushed to the floor by the crack of a bullet in his back. I eventually was able to sprint back to a defensive trench where there were eight or so men and I had a very brief moment to catch my breath and my thoughts. It was then that I could see the West Pier in flames and how many civilians, living and dead, hadn't fled in time, and I sobbed, I sobbed like a child until a nearby exploding shell brought me back round.

**How were you able to run with your injury?**

I don't know if you could call it running, I don't remember. Whether the adrenaline had kicked in, but I was going as fast as I could, that's all I know.

**Was there any moment you thought the battle could have been won?**

There was a brief moment; I remember the scream of a group of Spitfires strafing up and down the beach when I was in the trench and I thought the battle was turning, this didn't last long though, all of them had been shot down in one way or another within a few minutes. I spoke to the man next to me, but he was in a daze, I think he was still alive at that point but his neck seemed to be open, as if it were an open door. The men were firing, blindly it seemed, into the direction of the beach and I remember feeling completely exposed from all angles in that trench. It was only when we heard the rumblings of the tracks of Panzer Tanks that we decided to move, we saw one pull round the corner, and a moment where it just seemed to stare at us, and then it fired, sending smoke and debris into the air and landing just in front of us. 'Run, run!' one of the men shouted, and at that point at least four of them were taken out by German soldiers from one of the high-storey hotels, the one I was defending I think and we stumbled into a baker's shop.

We ran through the back of the building and could see the defences above us in the cliffs. There was hand to hand fighting going on everywhere, but we couldn't shoot without hitting our own men. It was the ferocity that shocked me, they were lunging at each other desperately with anything, bayonets, rifle stocks, bricks, stones, shovels. I saw a bunker burnt out by a jet of flame from a flamethrower, and screaming men running out and collapsing, it truly was hell on earth. These men must have been the parachutists from the night before.

We headed towards the town centre and there were only two of us left now, I was soon on my own when I turned round to notice the other soldier sobbing, kneeling down, looking for his left arm. I remember running around a corner to see another Panzer Tank staring at me, it shot just behind me and the wall of the building collapsed and landed on me, and for me, the Battle of Brighton, and the War, was over.

*What happened next?*

I woke up on my back inside the rear of an open field truck, travelling at speed down some muddy track. I couldn't see it; I could just feel it. I found myself back at Cambridge hospital believe it or not. It turned out that somehow, I had been blinded, I was honourably discharged by the army. I offered to stay on but they confessed they had no use for me. My current situation? Let's not discuss that, I suppose I should consider myself lucky I got out of Brighton alive, there are people much worse off than me. Still, I find it hard to be grateful for my current state.

**I've spoken to other veterans, and do forgive me for this, but their accounts of the battle are completely at odds with yours.**

Well, well war is what you see in front of you isn't it.

**Some people have said that your account – which you have given over and over to the press – is very like some war films which have done the rounds. What do you have to say to that?**

Bugger off.

**With that final riposte, Mr Sponge reached unerringly for the glass containing the dregs of his drink and left, turning at the door to greet an old**

comrade. For a blind person, he gets around almost miraculously well and his limp is often completely cured, if it isn't in his right leg or occasionally his left. This reporter was left to conclude that actually William Sponge – whose name occurs nowhere in the written record – is an actor of the first water and is rather wasting his time living as a down and out at the Colliery. [Legal – can you have a shufti at this for me before it goes to print, there's a dear.]*

*Ed: We believe this is a 'rough' draft of the article, which was never actually used in the newspaper.

WOT?
No WEAPONS &
DEFENCE?

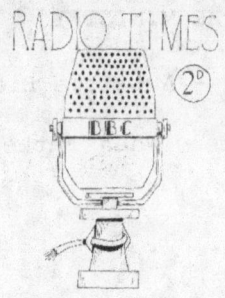

## Witford Radio - 1570kHz MW
*Putting the spunk back in Blighty*

Gracie Fields - Thing-Ummy-Bob

George Jackley - Ain't It Grand To Be Bloomin' Well Dead?

WEATHER REPORT

Charles Jolly - The Laughing Policeman
George Formby - A Farmer's Boy

EVACUATION UPDATES

Lily Morris - Don't Have Any More, Missus Moore

Florrie Forde - A Bird In A Gilded Cage

OBITUARIES

Bobby Comber - La Di Da Di Da

George Formby - Mother, What'll I Do Now

Richard Denham

UPDATES FROM THE MINISTRY
•
Harry Champion - A Little Bit Of Cucumber

Billy Williams - When Father Papered The Parlour

18

# THE WIDOW

Name: Catherine Lowe
Location: Trafford Grove, Manchester
Occupation: Retired
Threat level: 1
Article clearance: Bronze
Case file: 82/3235/GBW

It was a delight to meet Mrs Lowe, a woman who can quite honestly be called the salt of the earth. She lives alone now and is the last resident in the street where she brought up her family and where she was living when she sadly lost her husband. But she isn't bitter; she sees the best in every situation and if the Ministry had its wits about it, Mrs Lowe would be on posters the length and breadth of the country, as an example to all the weary Willies and tired Tims who are dragging our morale into the gutter. However, the best person to speak for the Mrs Lowes of this world is the lady herself.

How long have you lived on Trafford Grove Mrs. Lowe?

Must be forty years now, I would think. I've been a Manchester girl all my life. Reg was a cheeky chap on my street, always up to mischief, harmless mischief mind. He got a job in cotton when he left the school and I remember us being on the same bus home, we got chatting, and the rest is history! We moved here when I married Reg and I've always liked it, it was a lovely place. You could leave your front door open or unlocked and never have any bother. There was such a good community, we'd help each other out where we could, a few of the young lads would run errands to the shops for me if I asked, we even had the odd street party into the late hours. Oh I doubt there was anything unusual about my road really, it was probably the same up and down the country, wasn't it?

## Do you ever feel frightened or alone?

That's the thing, isn't it? It would probably be less odd if all of the other houses were boarded up or lying as ruins, but most of the houses are still intact on my road. You could be forgiven for thinking everyone has just gone away on holiday and will be back soon. If it wasn't for the odd bit of vandalism, smashed windows and graffiti scattered about you wouldn't have an inkling something was up. My neighbours may very well have every intention of coming back one day, I don't know. I have never seen any of them since as none have made a trip to come back and see their old homes.

I won't lie, I don't think there is any shame in it, but I have helped myself to supplies from the other houses, just to top up what I grow in the garden. I always make a note in my book of what I've taken from where, though, it was something Reg started, he's always been good like that. I make a note of everything I take and from where so I can pay the owners back if they ever return or when things go back to normal. Every now and then there's the odd tinker selling his wares too, young lads they are.

I like to go for a walk when my knees are up to it, it's quite ghostly, especially at night. How quiet it is, but the silly thing is, I suppose it's a bit like a graveyard, I can't ever work out if I find it scary and haunting or peaceful and serene. I don't venture too far though, there are a lot of bad sorts in the town centre, you can hear them from miles off. A lot of times I thought it was foxes, but it was actually people crying out due to whatever mischief they'd found themselves in.

## When did people start leaving?

Oh there was no one occasion that stands out, a lot of the children went in the government evacuations. Others left when they heard about Brighton, then Crawley. Out of forty or so families, half of them were still around, though. The atmosphere changed, people seemed to keep to themselves, they stopped trusting each other, doors were locked, heads kept low, a shame really, no need for any of that at all. I suppose most of them went when everyone on the road received some scaremongering nonsense from London through their door. By the end of that week, there was only me, Reg and one other family left.

## How did you feel when you realized you and your husband were the last people left on the street?

I remember the night where the last of ours neighbours, the Sealey family, moved out. Reg was out fishing or something like that I think, yes it must have been fishing. The Sealeys were in a complete panic bless their hearts. Mr. Sealey was always a nervous man, even before the troubles, he worked at the grocer's. People gossiped he saw some nasty stuff in the Great War to make him how he was, but we didn't delve, it would be improper for a war hero. He was banging on my door, 'Mrs. Lowe, Mrs. Lowe, come on we're getting out of here! We're not leaving you and Mr. Lowe behind!'. His face was white as snow, God only knows what had just happened, 'Where are you going to go?' I said. I tried to speak calmly and matter of fact, he was in that much of a fluster, pacing back and forth, 'I don't know, I don't know, somewhere safe!' 'You daft beggar,' I laughed, 'nowhere is safe. If you need to go I understand, but me and Reg are just fine.' The poor man shook his head and then paced off with his wife and three children in tow, all of them carrying suitcases and luggage. I'd love to know what happened to them.

When Reg came home he said his usual, 'Get the kettle on dear I'm back,' always made me chuckle that did. I told him the Sealey family had gone and I remember he just

tutted and said, 'Oh that's a shame, nice family they were.'
And in his way, he just beamed a broad smile and presented
his catch, fish for supper! We had our dinner, listened to the
wireless and then, you'll never believe it, Reg had a little
party for us, just the two of us, he was funny like that. He put
the gramophone on, 'Now is the hour' by Vera Lynn I think
it was. He was dressed up to the nines in his old uniform
from the Great War and he told me to get changed into my
Sunday finest. When I came back down, he'd somehow
come across a few bottles of wine and some whiskey. We got
through them all that night!

We cleared the living room table and just danced,
danced we did like two young love birds in each other's
arms, it was a lovely night. Somewhere in the distance we
could hear sirens but Reg, in that way he did, just laughed,
perhaps we were too drunk to care. Do you know what he
did? The silly beggar. He opened the windows to the living
room and blasted the music as loud as it would go, and he
handed me a gas mask. So there we were, two old buggers in
our best, in our gas masks, dancing in each other's arms in
an empty street while somewhere far away the skyline was
lighting up red, smoke was blowing down our road and the
sirens whined. What a sight we must have looked to anyone
if they saw us, but Reg and I didn't mind. It was a perfect
night, a lovely little memory for me to cherish.

**If you will forgive the question, when did Reg
pass?**

Oh don't be silly dear, I remember Reg was in the living
room and I was in the kitchen, he was shouting out to me
about 'the nonsense from Whitehall' he was reading at the
time. We heard the sound of clattering, like sticks rolling
across metal railings. Reg went outside to have a look and
there was a gang of half a dozen teenagers with their faces
covered with hessian sacks with mouth and eye holes so they
clearly weren't up to any good. They began moving into the
houses in pairs, smashing windows, kicking down doors

when they had to and helping themselves to whatever they found. Reg and I couldn't really judge I suppose; we'd done the same thing just in a politer way. Eventually they walked up to our house and Reg stood in the doorway, very polite but firm he was. 'Alright, lads, you've had your fun. You can carry on doing what you're doing, but not this house, we still live here.' The lads paused and mumbled between themselves, and began to walk off, much to our relief. One of them must have had a change of heart though because they came back and threw a stone through our front window, the noise was horrible. Reg ran out and told them to clear off, which they began to do, but again one of them then came running along and smacked Reg clear round the head with his staff. Reg collapsed to the floor, at least at that point they had the decency to run off.

I checked on Reg, and I'm no nurse, but he was gone. Had his age caught up with him, was it the strike alone, did his heart give in I don't know. I was bereft, distraught, I spent the whole day, alone on that street, cradling him in my arms, weeping as if I was his mother. Reg wasn't like that though, wasn't one to hold a grudge, he'd think his murderer was a daft kid rather than a monster. Even then I knew he was upstairs, God hopes, smiling on me and telling me to pull myself together.

I won't lie, I was in a daze, the world seemed completely silent, I walked, just walked, don't ask me why or where I was going but I eventually came across five lads working the land. Heaven knows how long I had been walking for. I told them that Reg was dead and they offered to bury him for me, for a sack of vegetables and some of his cigars. I wouldn't smoke them, filthy habit.

The lads were very kind and said they were sorry to hear my husband had been killed, I never told them that, but they must have guessed, word travels fast, don't it? They offered to take me in, they were based out of an old factory but I told them no, they'd have no use for me and I've had no use for them. No, Trafford Grove is my home. And that's that, I've been here alone for the last few years now.

## Would you ever consider evacuating your home?

Oh no, perish the thought. Too many happy memories I've got here and what on earth would I do elsewhere? No, no, I'm absolutely fine dear, I've had a good run and some lovely memories to keep me busy. It's the youngsters I feel sorry for; they'll never know the Manchester I did.

Oh yes sir, I joined the Church of the Remnant
voluntarily. I'm not desperate at all'
- *Southern Herald*

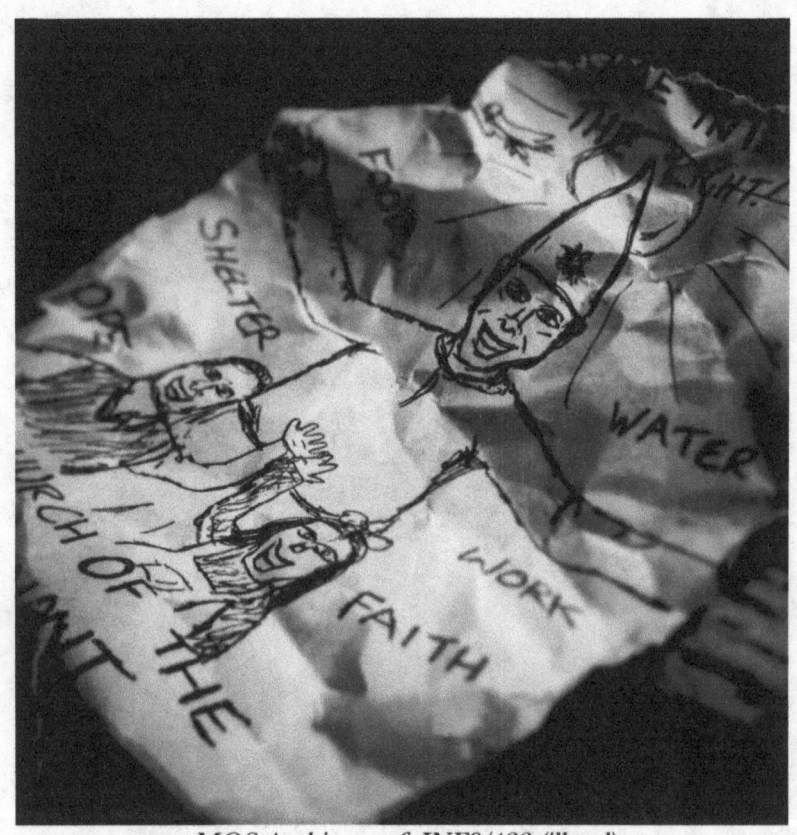

*MOS Archives, ref. INF9/422 (illegal)*

# THE REVEREND

Richard Denham

**Name: Alexander Green**
**Location: Hartley Wintney, Hampshire**
**Occupation: Vicar**
**Threat level: 4**
**Article clearance: Silver (amendment 2.4**
**applies)**
**Case file: 13/4563/GBR**

Regular readers of these pages will know that I
frown on overt religious beliefs, as I think that
everyone should be allowed to believe in just what
they please, when they please as long as they keep
it to themselves and don't do it in the street and
frighten the horses. That said, the Reverend Green
seems very dedicated and committed to his place
in our society as it functions nowadays, although a
bit less time spent pontificating on street corners
and a little bit more time helping people like last
weeks' interviewee might make us all feel less
ambivalent to the religious maniacs which infest
our country. [Legal – check please? Thanks; you're
a lamb]

Reverend Green, you were one of the few people to
witness the Church of the Remnant in the early
days without being a member. Can you explain
how that came about?

If truth be told, I don't even know where to start. I suppose
I should explain my background first, I was born in
Guildford and educated at Oxford University. I have been
Reverend of St. John's Church in Hartley Wintney, in
north east Hampshire for thirteen years now. Despite the
fact the A30 runs through the village, it is a quiet and

pleasant corner of England. Well, as quiet and pleasant as things can be nowadays. As a rural area, I am very grateful that the events of the Great Tribulation have not had such a devastating effect on my parishioners as had been experienced in other parts of the country. In fact, I suspect this village has endured very well, all things considered.

There were rumblings about The Church of the Remnant which were, in my view very foolishly, disregarded as a nonsense, a passing fad and a knee-jerk reaction to the events in Britain. The synod of the Church of England began emergency meetings in York and they were viewed as a secular problem. Then Archbishop Farthing declared that to acknowledge them was to legitimize them, and so they were to be ignored, as best as could be.

Do understand this wasn't taken lightly by those who were strongly opposed to the Remnant. Horror stories were shared, and we were all aware of the information on them that had been disseminated by the Ministry. Ultimately though, we had to respect the Archbishop's decision.

There was a fear behind the Remnant, the fact we were so ignorant of its motives, its leadership and above all, its ability to attract people to its flock. With my parishioners in the village, they would ask me about them and I would do my best to play it down. They were like the boogeymen some would say, who would steal children in the night; or who would lure desperate mothers and their babes into their ranks, never to be seen again.

The Synod continued to meet three times a year, a preposterously inadequate amount of time in hindsight. I remember that each time I arrived, a few people had disappeared, what had happened to them I do not know. Whether these men couldn't get there, had given up on the Church of England or perhaps even joined the Remnant I don't know. There was certainly a solemnity with the Archbishop, the last synod I attend there must have been but an eighth of those who were meant to be in attendance.

Archbishop Farthing announced his retirement then, and I simply stopped attending after that.

There were a handful of sightings of members of the Church, and there was nothing covert about their operation. I remember one Saturday the sound of a bell ringing out from the street while I was in the church grounds, I walked over to the A30 and saw a line of two dozen or so people walking eastwards. They were mainly women, children and the elderly and they looked in a pathetic and sorry state, but they seemed to be there voluntarily. A crowd of villagers had come to watch the peculiar spectacle, and they were clearly as dumbstruck as I was as to how to respond. It was hard to know if the gathered crowd would throw rotten vegetables, hurl obscenities or offer the group food and water; in the end they did none of these things and simply watched in silence as the group passed. The bell-ringer appeared to be in a daze I must say, quoting obscure lines from the bible, I can only assume these were people looking to join the Church of the Remnant.

Beyond this handful of occasions, nothing much happened in Hartley Wintney. A few months passed and eventually Bishop Timms of Winchester, essentially my boss, arrived at St. John's with a couple of his men. I assumed he was going to castigate me for failing to attend the synod. However, after the formalities were out of the way, to my surprise he did not even mention it.

**What did you discuss?**

Bishop Timms is a man I admired, he was a mentor to me. I remember him talking to me in private in my study about the Church of the Remnant, delicately aiming the conversation in a way to gauge my thoughts on them. It was clear he was weighing something up in his mind. I answered him honestly and explained that they are an unknown quantity, yes, I had heard the rumours but they were just that. Eventually, Bishop Timms opened up and explained he had been invited to visit Guildford Cathedral in Surrey, which had been 'acquired' by the Remnant. What exactly that meant, who is to say? The Cathedral was still in the hands of Bishop Greendale, so I would assume some sort of defection to the Remnant.

I had met Bishop Greendale, and I was surprised to learn he had defected, if indeed that was what it was. Bishop Timms talked excitedly of a new era and the revitalization of the Church, I remember him talking of the Senators and Landowners in Gaul during the Roman times, how they embraced the Roman Church lest they be destroyed by it. How they successfully rode the wave of change, and manoeuvred to keep themselves in power, simply ruling in God's name rather than the Emperor's. He told us this is what we must do, if we were to have any future.

We discussed all these matters into the early hours in my study, broken up only by the smoking of cigars or the drinking of brandy, which I'm ashamed to say I have acquired quite a taste for now. Eventually I agreed to travel with Bishop Timms the next day to Guildford Cathedral, I was determined to go in with an open mind. Bishop Timms still had a working Rover P12 which one of his men drove.

**What was different about the Cathedral when you arrived?**

In terms of the building itself? Nothing. The land around the Church had a vast number of farm-hands and there appeared to be the early processes of several rings of walls being established, but nothing of concern. We drove up to the main road, where we were greeted by a gate-keeper, pleasant enough, he announced that Bishop Greendale was expecting us and could we make the remainder of the journey on foot if we would be so kind. It was only when I was out of the vehicle and close enough to see the workers themselves that something felt odd.

**Can you describe what the followers of the Church wear?**

Followers of the Church became known as Dunsmen, due to the very bizarre and theatrical conical hats they wear, similar to a dunce cap you would find in a school. One can speculate on the purpose or symbolism of these hats, but it is clearly some odd reference to being repentant or slow-learners, or deserving of punishment. It's not something I'm willing to give too much thought too, though I can't imagine their hats are particularly practical for labouring and agricultural work. The hats also appear to range in size, which again, I am sure has some inner-meaning.

The majority of Dunsmen also wear rough woollen tunics over their normal clothes, which looks absolutely ridiculous to a modern eye. There seems to be a variation in that women wear longer ones than men and children, but that is the only thing notable to me.

Now, I would like nothing more to tell you, that the Dunsmen were all brain-washed, mindless drones going about their work in silence but I would be lying to you. By all means, there is a fanatical element there, but although I was forbidden from talking to them directly, it was easy to overhear their conversations as they worked in the fields and built their timber structures, it was nothing peculiar in the main, and the sort of thing you'd have heard on any street corner or market place. If the Church was made up solely of these people, it would seem nothing but a harmless, if eccentric, communal estate.

The fellows that were very foreboding and ominous, though, wore red cones, and dressed head to toe in the colour. I am aware the red dunsmen have been referred to as prefects, but I never heard that title being used myself. Their faces are all covered, but they strangely only have an eye hole for their right eyes, a very odd sight. You understand this is all conjecture on my part, but I would guess they exist in some sort of security role. They travel in groups of four or so, armed with sickles and scythes, appearing to patrol the Church land. I heard no conversation, casual or otherwise from these men. They were watching over a group of Dunsmen who were busy building a perimeter wall in a rather ugly and haphazard fashion. A mixture of sheet metal, timber, brick and ruins from other buildings. One point they were even using a burnt out double decker to build around. A rather ugly blight on the countryside.

Although all members of the Church wore bizarre outfits to my eyes, the most ridiculous were reserved for the masters. Their outfits can be best described as a devilish hybrid of head-master attire and for reasons beyond my comprehension, also the long white horsehair wigs worn by judges, these men, all of them are men, carry canes with them. To my eyes, they looked like pantomime characters, I was expecting them to burst out into song at any moment, but I would have been the only one who found it amusing I fear.

Bishop Timms and I were eventually lead into Greendale's office, where he was waiting for us, and despite all we had seen, he was dressed in his normal attire. That to me, was the most absurd part, that he was not partaking in the theatricality, despite him being I assume, the leader there.

Bishop Greendale remained as pleasant and unassuming as ever, articulate and wise, and I was treated well by him. I remained an observer to most of the conversation between the two men. The two men spoke in private for the last hour and Bishop Timms eventually collected me, we returned to Hartley Wintney and then he and his two men continued to Winchester. As simple as that.

**Could you tell me what was discussed?**

I would prefer not to, I'm afraid. I do not believe it would be right. I do not wish to get into a long conversation about theology but I must confess that despite all their odd

practices and their theatrical appearance, they are building a strong, cohesive and workable society – and the suffering of other survivors is largely unknown to The Church. Whether they are a force for good or evil will be for history to decide, I suppose. Whatever can and should be said about them, they do welcome everyone, even if those that join them are only the most desperate and lost, they do indeed welcome them, and that must be to their favour. There is a simplicity to the Church, and if I dare to risk condemning my soul, I would suppose that their form of Christianity is much more Christian than mine. They work the land, work as one, one voice, one community, they dedicate their lives to sustenance and to prayer. They follow the good book to the letter, and everything that implies. Yes, they may be sinister, and I suspect there is much more to them that I have seen, but I admit, if Jesus were to return, he would most likely understand the motives of the Church of the Remnant than he would the Church of England. For though I will say our Church is much more human, compassionate and patient, it cannot be denied that, from a historical point of view, ours is an apostasy, a pleasant one, but an apostasy none the less.

**There are many reports of intimidation, violence and criminality within the Church of the Remnant, how do you respond to that?**

As I have previously mentioned, I have seen none of it myself. That is not to say that it hasn't happened, or I do not believe it, but it would be wrong of me to judge and comment on things I do not know to be true. Do not mistake me for a fool though, I know the stories of people having their tongues cut out who speak against the Dunsmen, writers who lose their fingers, homes being burnt, women being forced to reproduce with the masters, but what can I say. The old world is dead, the Church of England is dead, whatever the Church of the Remnant are doing, it is working, their numbers grow in scores and their fervour and determination only grows. Does the bible not say that 'the meek shall inherit the Earth?', then perhaps they are the meek.

**What happened after the meeting?**

A few months passed and one of Bishop Timms' men returned again, this time by horse. He asked me my views on the Church of the Remnant, I tried my best to articulate that I am a reverend of the Anglican Church, and it would be wrong for me to turn my back on the people of the village. The man simply nodded and passed on Bishop Timms' regards; I never saw the Bishop again. Though the rumour is that he too has now defected to the Church of the Remnant, whether or not this is at Winchester Cathedral I do not know.

**What are your plans for the future?**

As for me, I shall continue my work at St. John's, preaching to my dwindling congregation, the half a dozen or so souls that have not yet lost faith. What will happen to the Church after I have gone I do not know. That is for God to decide.

**My final question to the reverend gentleman whether he had, covertly, joined the Remnant, remained unanswered. All he would do was pray, increasingly loudly, as he ushered me out of the building. Although, as regular readers will know, I have not set foot in a place of worship since my last marriage – of which we will say no more – I know enough to know that none of the words were part of any Church of England service I have ever attended. In fact, if anything, it sounded a little reminiscent of the aforementioned street-corner preachers. But I will leave my readers to decide on the significance of that ...**

WOT?
NO BIBLICAL
QUOTATIONS?

*MOS Archives, ref. INF9/854 (endorsed)*

# THE HOUSEWIFE

Richard Denham

# THE HOUSEWIFE

Richard Denham

Name: Anne Routy
Location: Port Isaac, Cornwall
Occupation: Homemaker
Threat level: 1
Article clearance: Silver
Case file: 76/9564/GBW

I travelled with some difficulty down to Port Isaac to interview Anne Routy, a widow with two children. She lives in what some would consider idyllic surroundings, the archetypal cottage with roses around the door. Her garden is full of flowers and vegetables, with not an inch wasted. Down in a corner, screened from the house, there are chickens and – when the wind is in the right direction – it is clear that there is also a pig. With the sky a bright and cloudless blue and the cries of seagulls filling the crisp air from the sea, it is easy to forget the occurrences of recent times. Mrs Routy is not a native of these parts and her story is an interesting one.

**Mrs. Routy, thank you for talking to me. I understand you and your late husband were originally from London? How did you end up in Port Isaac?**

Oh it was terrible wasn't it, what was 'appening in London, we knew we had to get away from it all. After The Battle of Crawley, we knew we 'ad to get out while we still could. Robin and I were extremely lucky you see. 'e had family 'ere in Port Isaac and 'e 'ad a promise of work as a fisherman from 'is cousin under the very kind Mr. Shipham, so we left as soon as we could with the kids. I wasn't scared really, I suppose I was actually quite excited, the kids saw it as an adventure and that rubbed off on me. Oh, me and Robin 'ad our problems, as all couples do and Cornwall was a fresh start for us all.

## Did it take you long to adapt to your new life?

Oh not at all; Robin 'ad worked in a factory and always talked off 'ow much 'e 'ated it, so in some ways this work was like a 'oliday to 'im. The lads in the village were very kind and 'e was paired up with his cousin who taught 'im the ropes, pardon the pun!

We were assigned to a vacant cottage, this place you're in now as a matter of fact. The owner 'ad died with no next of kin and it was all part of the Ministry's re'ousing initiative. I'll always be grateful that we were one of the early lucky ones, we struck gold really. Obviously our 'ouse in London was forfeit, but that's probably rubble now anyway, isn't it? We were very lucky, the teachers at the school insisted on carrying on as normal so that kept the children busy too.

For me, it was more of the same really, a woman's work is the same anywhere. The women-folk of Port Isaac are a different stock to those in London but we soon became friendly enough and good neighbours. They even baked us cakes to welcome us and taught us some tricks on 'ow to manage our allotment and garden.

The children loved it too really, some days they'd complain it was quiet or they were bored, and there was none of the brouhaha back in the East-end but they soon adapted, when they were told stories of how other children 'ad it they soon became grateful.

## Have you been able to sustain yourself and your family?

Oh, yes, my love, of course. The good thing about fishing is there is something to fish all year round, Pilchards from July to November, 'erring from November to January, January to July is mackerel and up until April you've got flatfish, ray, conga and skate, you get the idea. Port Isaac is a fisherman's dream, Robin never 'ad to worry about 'auling up his boat on the tide, the 'arbour wall kept it safe from the rough seas.

Mr. Shipham often discussed the changes to 'is suppliers and I suppose the lack of them, but it certainly didn't seem to affect anyone in the village too much. Things became more local, money stopped being such a concern and things were often paid in services or bartered rather than paid for, but I suppose unless you are well off you wouldn't notice the difference much.

**How has the community here responded to national events?**

Oh yes, there's be some 'orrible stories elsewhere hasn't there? People starving in the cities, riots, looting. Makes you wonder why the government can't get their act together. At first, most of Port Isaac's catch was requisitioned by the government, which was fine, the men didn't mind doing their bit. Gradually though, these trips got less and less, and we certainly weren't going to go out of our way to 'and it over unless we were asked too. Sometimes the men did go into town to find out what was going on but would often appear to come back more confused than when they left.

The town 'all was also concerned about attracting too many evacuees too, the first waves we could put to work on the boats or on the land, but gradually we 'ad to start turning people away, which could often end up quite unpleasant as you can imagine. We formed a town watch after the first few scuffles, eventually we found it easier to turn folk away before they got too near the village. This did make me and Robin feel very guilty really, the only difference between them and us was the fact we 'ad got 'ere a year or so earlier.

**Could you explain the circumstances before the incident involving your late husband?**

Robin was such a good 'onest man, oh, 'e enjoyed his drink, but what man doesn't? 'e was just doing his shifts for Mr. Shipham, funny old name that isn't it, for someone who works with boats. It was shellfish season, I remember that, summer it was, Robin would always take an extra crab pot for luck, not that 'e ever 'ad much, mind! The potting grounds were about a mile from shore. 'e had a good 'aul though, three dozen crabs. 'e'd always return 'ome late afternoon when 'e 'ad been with the crabs. 'e did 'ave a temper on 'im, so I'd always 'ave to make sure 'is dinner was ready for 'im on time or it could cause quite the upset.

Sometimes, and it's awful to say, but I'd like it when 'e was doing pilchards, because that's a night-time job, and it'd give Robin a chance to calm down and sober up. 'e'd leave just before sunset in pilchard season and not be back until morning. Mr. Shipham would come and visit me now and then, just to check in and make sure everything was alright. It was a lovely sunny day; the village was bustling with daily life. The men were drying out their fishing nets on the 'arbour wall ready for tanning. I was 'anging out the washing, a woman's work is never done is it? Each day a trip to the market and a rummage through the allotment and I wasn't expecting Robin until the morning.

I remember one morning there was a terrible commotion by the front door, I was still in bed and Robin 'ad come in with a couple of other lads and some injured chap who was 'alf drowned and 'alf naked, unconscious too. They explained they'd pulled him from a life raft a few miles out. We reported this to the town 'all but they didn't really seem to take much of an interest, believing him to just be another refugee and, I'll always remember this, they gave us 'permission to do as our conscience and the current circumstances see fit'.

'e was a young man, more of a child really, 'e 'ad a lovely smile on him. We nursed this man back to 'ealth in the spare bedroom, over several weeks, 'e couldn't say more than thank you to us, bless 'is 'eart. 'ere is the thing though, we eventually realized, he was a Jerry, if you can believe it! 'e couldn't communicate with us and no one in the village spoke German. Robin didn't know what to do, 'e reported it again to the town 'all but again, for reasons I'll never understand, they didn't seem interested, they suggested giving him a row-boat to make 'is way back across the Channel but the poor blighter was in no condition for that. We nicknamed him Jerry and despite what was going on, we trusted him, he helped out with the allotment and was always willing to work. The neighbours thought it odd that we 'ad 'im, like some sort of pet, but we explained we had reported it and were waiting to be told what to do, we thought the army would come to collect him at some point but they never did.

I remember one day Mr. Shipham came over, 'e thought the whole thing was quite amusing really, and brought round some paper and pencils. I think Jerry must 'ave knocked 'is 'ead though or was still ill as 'e never seemed quite there. Mr. Shipham gave Jerry the pencil in the 'ope 'e could draw or explain what 'ad 'appened to him. Eventually Jerry drew what we could tell was the English Channel, with a big boat where we were. 'e then drew a line around the map with the words 'Ring Aus Stahl' and what we think were battleships and landmines. An arrow pointed to one of the battleships near us.

'Well that's it' Robin said, 'e's obviously from the German navy. I don't think we'd be doing ourselves any favours if anything happens to Jerry, we should return 'im. Who knows, we might even get rewarded.' Mr. Shipham and Robin had a 'eated debate about the blockade, but Robin thought, if he took 'im out, in a rowing vessel, with a big white flag, everything would be ok. Jerry was obviously oblivious to this conversation. Eventually, Mr. Shipham agreed to let Robin take one of 'is rowing boats out.

Robin didn't waste any time, 'e dressed Jerry up for the journey and took 'im to the 'arbour and out into the boat, 'e'd brought with 'im a white-bed sheet as a flag and Mr. Shipham and I saw 'im off. Mr. Shipham said 'e'd stay at mine that night to make sure I was ok until Robin returned.

**What happened next?**

I don't know really. As they set off, Jerry seemed to be protesting and trying to grab the oars as if to turn round but Robin overpowered 'im; then I remember the drone of a fighter plane some minutes later. Robin and Jerry were soon turning into a dot on the 'orizon but I remember the plane circled several times, we guessed 'e was checking out the boat but then, would you believe it, it began firing its machine guns onto the boat! The poor men didn't stand a chance and the boat sank, the bodies were never recovered.

**That must have been awful, I'm sorry.**

Oh it was years ago now love, this sort of thing 'appens in war. There were lots of guesses by the men at what 'ad 'appened, but I'll tell you this, the men are careful about going too far out to sea now! Anyway life for me is fine, and we're doing well, Mr. Shipham is looking after us – in fact, I better run soon, 'e's taking me to the dance tonight!

**Like so much of life these days, it seems down in Port Isaac, it is a case of least said, soonest mended. And I did come home with a lovely hamper of fresh vegetables, newly laid eggs and some bacon. The pilchards were a nice thought, but I swapped those in the first pub I came to that was still open on the way home; they could do with something to supplement the bar snacks and I was**

**just desperate after all that fresh sea air for a nice stiff gin.**

# ATTENTION!

# ADVANCE WARNING.

# PORT ISAAC IS NO LONGER ACCEPTING OUTSIDERS. WE DO NOT HAVE ENOUGH FOOD TO FEED OUR OWN! MOVE ALONG.

# GO BEYOND THIS SIGN AT YOUR PERIL.

# PORT ISAAC CIVIL COMMITTEE

WOT?
NO FOOD
(IN THE WILD)?

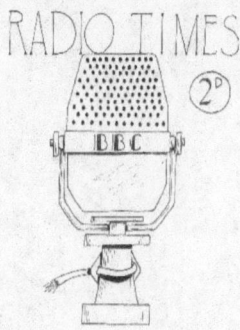

'Wathmere calling, Wathmere calling. A betrayal, a betrayal I denounce, of the most despicable. Where words and noise clang like iron and steel, forged into weapons on the great anvil of lies. To make a mockery of the great halls and pull back the curtains and for what? Do you wish to applaud you fools? Applaud the masks and the dances and think not on their meaning or their purpose. Parade me then like a perverse Aesop, parade me and let me be your whipping boy. Let the blood on the cobbled streets be my signature, let the ash and smoke rise in my likeness if that is what you must believe. Peace, peace is the sound that cannot be overheard by jeering mobs and screaming babes. Vile and odious it must seem, dire, dire, and may clarity reach you when the moans have quietened and the raging seas calmed. Are we the architects of our own design, or but pathetic and pitiful reeds that blow and bend in violent storms?

- Earl Wathmere, BUS Radio

# THE ENTREPRENEUR

**Name: Sir Montgomery Brown**
**Location: London**
**Occupation: [omitted]**
**Threat level: [omitted]**
**Article clearance: [omitted]**
**Case file: [omitted]**

Interviewing Sir Montgomery Brown is not easy. First, one must get past his small army of minders and secretaries and then into his home in Kensington, which is fortified to an extreme and some may say excessive degree. I was marched, at rifle point, into his presence having been searched by a none-too-gentle woman guard. The following interview has been checked by Sir Montgomery's staff, although I have since been able to add back in things which I had managed to jot down on my cuff. To avoid unduly influencing my readers, I have not indicated these sections – see if you can tell for yourself. Finally, if I disappear, or anything happens to me, I would like to tell my entire readership that Sir Montgomery and his entourage should be where any investigations, should any be allowed, must begin.

**Sir Montgomery, what attracted you to the British Union of Survivors?**

Before I start it is important to remember that the BUS in the early days compared to what you see now were very different animals. The Black-shirt thugs, who are fortunately now a minority, are unrecognisable in their ideals and methods from the BUS' foundations. As often happens to well-meaning ideas, as history teaches us, it was hijacked by violent men.

After the Battle of Crawley, there was a national outcry for peace, myself included; I wanted peace with the Reich. The war was clearly a lost cause; how many more men would have to die before we sued for peace? How much unnecessary suffering would there be before the inevitable defeat?

We must remember that the British government were the aggressors in this conflict. We started the war. I don't believe that the Reich would have fought Blighty at all if our warmongering politicians did not instigate it. After the siege of Redhill, well, that was the last roll of the dice wasn't it and Westminster truly had its tail between its legs after that.

Fortunately, diplomacy of a sort between Westminster and The Reich continued. The Reich knew all about the BUS and was well aware there was a movement among the populace for an end to the war. Many of the party members, including Earl Wathmere, had meetings with the German High Command, which I believe was a great aid to the later peace and ending of any further aggression.

As for me, at the time all this was going on I was a City banker, and an extremely successful one at that. If there is one thing the world of finance needs, it is order, and calm, and war, although profitable in its way, wasn't good for business. I had served in the Great War, and have experienced first-hand the absolute madness of it all. I was mortified when my sons were called up. Whatever the costs and sacrifice of peace, it was better than war. Whatever it took to pull my children out of that would be worth it.

I had friends in high places, and they introduced me to leading figures within the BUS. Their message of peace resonated with me and I was soon attending party rallies and became a paid-up party member. Due to my fortunate financial position I became one of the party's most generous donors. I was soon awarded a position on the committee as a result.

## Sir Montgomery, how well did you know Earl Wathmere?

I wouldn't say I knew him, not on any personal level. He was one of those sorts who stood out in any room, one of those charismatic men who became caricatures of themselves. Such an articulate and amusing man; well, his were speeches that everyone wanted to hear. In terms of his political stance, he was a moderate, but his way with words would convince anyone of anything, I believe.

## How did Earl Wathmere become involved with the BUS?

There was of course a growing faction within Westminster sympathetic to the BUS and hoping for peace with The Reich. To the warmongers in government, this was most divisive and infuriating. After Operation Sea Lion this minority of Ministers simply became too large and loud to ignore. Earl Wathmere left the incumbent government and joined the BUS, much to our delight, and it was Wathmere's defection that really made us a force to be reckoned with. Do remember though, Wathere was simply a well-known and recognisable member of the party, not the party itself, as others may have you believe. People seem to forget the party had been around a long time before Wathmere joined. With him, the BUS ranks swelled, the Black-shirts, as they had been nicknamed, were well and truly here to stay.

I don't believe he had any desire or ambitions to become Party leader. I believe it was something that just happened. He was far too powerful and admired by the public not to be. Wathmere was very much caught on the tide of success rather than being master of the seas directing those waves. Earl Wathmere was also a very influential media mogul, he owned the Southern Herald newspaper among many others, so he became a very effective cog in promoting the BUS machine to the nation.

I remember Wathmere was always quite uncomfortable about being coerced into saying and championing ideas that were not his own. I don't believe he was ever comfortable with the particularly militant style the black shirts of the BUS had adopted. He had grave concerns that the Black-shirts were in his words 'A ravenous wolf that grows in strength, our tether weakens and soon it shall snap. And that wolf will no longer be under our control. It will be feral and deadly, so please, let us not feed this beast any further'.

Tensions between the Government and the BUS party grew more and more strained. It wasn't until the second battle of Cable Street, and all that nasty business that followed with the police, that civilities well and truly broke down. Earl Wathmere was declared an enemy of the crown by Downing Street and the BUS party were banned as a treasonous faction. A national amnesty was declared but those who ignored this would be dealt with in the harshest manner. The party continued to meet, albeit in more clandestine ways. Wathmere went into hiding, and there were more than enough powerful people sympathetic to him that he was able to continuously move from place to place, out of the reach of the Government and always one step ahead of the police.

This outlawing of Earl Wathmere didn't have the effect the Government planned, though. Actually, it was quite the opposite. He wasn't viewed as an outcast, a criminal or a deviant. Instead he became somewhat of a martyr figure, a persecuted hero, a Robin Hood character of sorts. A champion of peace against a perverse and warmongering Government that was marching Britain into oblivion.

The Black-shirt movement continued to grow, and as Wathmere prophesised, the tether snapped. Now, to reiterate, it's important to distinguish between the BUS party and the Black-shirts, no matter how hard that seems. The Black-shirts were an unruly mob, a beacon to the most violent, thuggish and criminal sorts. They had a couple of nicknames that did amuse me, 'the red bus' on account of their violence, and the 'double deckers', again a pun on the acronym.

**As a party member of the British Union of Survivors, how did all this affect you?**

With the dissolution of the BUS, there was no control over the Black-shirts, none at all. Obviously, BUS had been banned, and the Government could enforce this among the politicians. However, on the street, against the Black-shirts, they simply didn't have the manpower or resources to effectively police this, and there were too many men at all levels sympathetic enough to turn the other way. The Black-shirts saw themselves as an heroic and persecuted faction against a corrupt government and the tit-for-tat attacks and reprisals simply escalated the violence and anarchy. The Black-shirts were beyond the control of both the BUS and the Government. Westminster really began to take this matter very seriously indeed. After the riots and the Battle of Westminster Bridge, the Government began to negotiate with former members of BUS in secret to try to find a way to end the madness.

**Could you explain what was discussed at these secret meetings?**

No, no, never.

**Did you meet Earl Wathmere again?**

Yes, on several occasions, in fact. His time on the run had changed him drastically, though; he was unrecognisable, both in appearance and temperament. He was clearly very distressed about what was happening, despairing almost. It affected him greatly, he had sleepwalked into becoming the symbol and figurehead of the Black-shirts; a messianic figure for a cause that not only did he not agree with but actually opposed. The riots of Liverpool and Glasgow, the great fire of Lincoln. He was demonised by the government for this, who were always quick to lay the blame at his door, but he had no involvement, none at all, he had no part in any of it.

He pleaded with the committee to allow him to stand down or resign, but they refused, he was simply too entrenched in the movement now to be allowed to walk away. Over the following months, Wathmere became increasingly isolated, hiding away, going days, weeks without seeing anyone. He turned to drink, and some would whisper to madness, in his grief and despair.

## What happened next?

That's the darnedest and most confusing thing. The Government had realised he was losing his mind and they used this to their diabolic advantage. I don't really know what or how it happened, only the Government at the time do, but somehow one of their men was able to infiltrate the BUS movement and befriended Wathmere. The agent pretended he was sympathetic to him. He told Wathere that he was part of a faction within the party that wanted to turn away from violence and disassociate themselves from the Black-shirts and they arranged to move Wathmere to a secret estate.

Wathmere eventually agreed, and travelled at night with the Agent to the estate, the location of which no one except that Government knows of course.

And here is the most despicable thing in my mind, the Government prayed on his deteriorating mental health, grief and despair. They announced they were creating the British Union of Survivors radio, and Earl Wathmere was to be the host. This was despicable for two reasons, firstly, Earl Wathmere genuinely believed these men were on his side, they would encourage him to ramble and spurt nonsense and applaud him for it, allowing and I suspect encouraging him to be in drink and making him think that they and the public were on his side. Secondly, the whole purpose of this was for his broadcasts to show the country what a nonsense he was, and to cheapen the BUS at the same times.

## It worked didn't it?

Yes, yes, very well, in fact, way beyond the Government's wildest dreams, I'd imagine. Earl Wathmere became a laughing-stock, countless people would tune into his drunken broadcasts. The BUS tried to distance themselves from him but it didn't work. Over time, BUS gradually fell apart into various local factions and began to crumble from within. There was, and still is, a fanatical element who remained loyal to Wathmere, but this dwindling minority remain well and truly on the fringes.

The Ministry still operate BUS radio to this day, and Earl Wathmere must be nothing more than a prisoner to them. I have heard rumours that he lives his life in his study, with his radio equipment, locked away from the outside world. If this is true I don't know, but it wouldn't surprise me and as you know, Wathmere is undoubtedly beyond the ability to understand or escape his situation.

## Do you regret the fall of the BUS?

I'd be so bold to say I believe you'd be surprised to know how many former BUS members made up the XXII committee and the Ministry from there. So, in a bizarre way, with the peace, the BUS, and particularly Earl Wathmere, got what he wanted after all. The tragedy being though I doubt the Earl is even aware...

## What is your current situation?

Come now, that's not what we are discussing is it? Let's just say I've remained very pragmatic with my loyalties. I'm very comfortable still here in London, and I have enough fingers in different pies for that to continue for the foreseeable future. Gentleman such as I will always endure. Money still talks, and always will...

**You say the Black-shirts were disbanded and the BUS distanced themselves from them, but aren't the men guarding your house Black-shirts?**

Be careful, I don't want you asking questions you don't want to hear the answer too. Anyone who has the sense and money has personal security don't they? And their uniforms my men wear, there not really black are they? More of a dark navy...

Anyway, I'd like to end this interview now. I have a soiree on Great Smith Street to attend tonight.

'Just smile comrades and hopefully no one will mention
Wind-bag at our party conference in Margate...'
- *Southern Herald*

*MOS Archives, ref. INF9/547 (endorsed)*

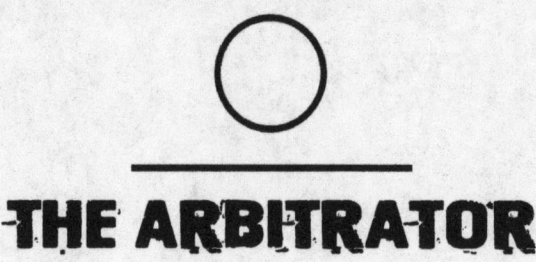

# THE ARBITRATOR

(Picture omitted)

**Name: Cyril Sopwith**
**Location: (omitted)**
**Occupation: Adjudicator**
**Threat level: 1**
**Article clearance: Silver (amendment 6.5 and 9.1**
**applies)**
**Case file: (omitted)**

NOTE: THIS IS AN UNEDITED AND
UNAPPROVED ARTICLE

Unfortunately I failed to interview Mr. Sopwith for
reasons which I hope become clear as you read on.
Here are my notes from that very peculiar day and
I shall let you decide what to do with them, let me
know if you have any questions, though I'm just
not sure I'll have any answers!

I had been invited to interview Mr. Cyril Sopwith,
who is an adjudicator for (omitted), a private club
for (omitted) in (omitted) affectionately known by
its attendees as Aunt Sally's. My regular readers
will have to forgive my obscure writing and
vagueness, this has been for no reason, honest or
otherwise, simply than for the fact I was not, and
am not actually aware of what I witnessed that
strange day. I had been invited as a guest to attend
the day and was asked to dress in formal wear. So,
dressed to the nines I attend (omitted) where I
handed over my invitation to a doorman, who
scowled at it before allowing me inside.

**Inside Aunt Sally's is a great Georgian Hall. Two impossibly large renaissance oak tables run the length of the vast room. At the far end is a dais with a large set of beautifully carved weighing scales, twice the size of a man. Beyond that there is a straw man, assumedly the mascot of (omitted), wearing a crown and a strange mask that appears to blend the two operatic faces of comedy and tragedy. A velvet rope cordons off the area which marks my threshold as a visitor, so I am resigned to a small visitor's bar at the end as I watch a multitude of elderly men in tuxedos arrive for the day's... whatever it is.**

**Eventually the Hall is full with these gentlemen and recognising Cyril among them would be impossible, the din of mindless conversation echoing in the room is almost unbearable and I am tempted to leave until a figure arrives at the dais and slams his gavel down, which I assume to be Mr. Sopwith. It is a strain to hear what is being said over the noise of the distinguished mob.**

'Order, order. Welcome one and all.' The figure declares.

'And all and one', the mob repeats in unison which is followed with a chorus of self-appreciating laughter.

'First up is Mr. Singh'.

'Shame, shame' the mob bellows in a low-pitched mantra as a confused man walks onto the stage.

'Now, now gentleman. He's entitled to have his say isn't he?' Sopwith patronisingly announces to his colleagues. 'So, Mr. Singh, what *do* you have to say?'.

Mr. Singh steps forward and begins to give his piece but it is impossible to hear a word as the crowd break-out into small talk. The look on the man's face becomes increasingly despondent as he realises no one can or is listening to him and his attempts to speak over the chatter are hopeless.

'Well… there you have it chaps.' Sopwith said as the crowd returns to a reasonable level of quiet. 'So who will start me off?'

A strange and unusual ritual then begins, which despite my best efforts, I am unable to translate. One at a time an attendee rises from the table and shouts out a Latin term or some bizarre esoteric phrase, met with varying degrees of appreciation or opposition by the crowd based on the volume of their grunting.

'Habeas corpus!' one declares, he then walks up to the giant weighing scales in front of the dais and places an amount of money in one of the scales, tipping it slightly to the left, to the excitement of all.

A second figure stands, shaking his head. 'Hereby, henceforth, herewith' before himself proceeding to place a larger amount of money in the second scale.

'A priori' the third weasel-faced gentleman announces to much laughter. 'Ad quod damnum. De minimis non curat lex.' The man then walks over the scale and makes a game of pretending which scale he is going to go to, appearing to change his mind several times, before placing it in the left scale.

Mr. Singh appears to be the only other person than me and the barman in the room who isn't entertained, let alone understanding, of what is happening.

'On the contrary!' a fourth figure cries, 'Not so, not so. Did it not?'. This statement appears to attract some minor protest from the attendees, which is drowned out with raucous applause when the man places a large amount of money into the right scale. Tipping it down.

'Anymore for anymore?' Sopwith calls out. 'Well there you are Mr. Singh. No more for no more. Argumentum ad populum.' Mr. Singh looks around confused as he is ushered off the stage to polite clapping.

The obstreperous din returns as servants begin to arrive with trays of champagne for the gentlemen. I use this opportunity to refill my own glass and speak to the barman. 'Can you tell me? What is going on.'

The barman appears reluctant to speak to me or make eye contact, 'It's their way' he mumbles as he pours me another gin.

'But *what* is going on?' I ask, only to be met with a shake of the head and the barman disappearing from the counter.

After a brief break for refreshments, the affairs begin again as a clearly distressed mother and her teenage daughter are brought onto the stage. 'Contempt? Contempt?', Sopwith jokes to his listeners to quiet them down as they return to their seats at the table. 'Mrs and Miss Gwent, and what would *you* like to say?'

'For shame! Shame on you all!' Mrs. Gwent calls out which is only met by bass laughter, her subsequent words cannot compete with the noise and she gives up her protest after a few minutes, exasperated.

'Starter for ten?' Sopwith tentatively asks.

'Starter for nine!' a heckle shouts out back, met with ecstatic applause.

The surreal spectacle begins again as various men rise from their seat, shout their words, and place money on the scale.

'Per contra!'

'Not so. Forthwith. Against all thoughts.'

'Prima facie! Pro hac vice.'

'Compellingly so, alas not.'

'Qui facit per alium, facit per se.'

'Much thought and scant regard.'

One gentleman puts an equal amount of money in each scale, cancelling itself out, which is congratulated with the rhythmic thumping on fists on the tables. However, this act is soon forgotten as a final man calls out 'Res gestae', before placing an obscene amount of money into the left scale, apparently bringing the *thing* to an end.

There is an emotional scene as the mother and daughter are ripped out of each other's arms and taken off the dais in opposite directions. The sadness of this is missed by the audience who have returned to their feet to begin mingling again as further champagne is brought out. The gentlemen, who moments ago appeared to be in violent opposition to each other are now the best of friends.

I return to the visitor's bar, where I finally notice I am the only person on this side of the velvet rope and I hand my glass to the barman. I have a thousand questions which it is clear by the man's eyes he has no intention of answering, in the end I can simply smile to myself and ask for another gin. The pattern of the ritual begins yet again as after ten minutes or so Sopwith returns. 'Mr. Oakbridge please', he calls out as a member of the audience walks up to the stage and shakes Sopwith's hand. The crowd go deathly silent and after a moment Sopwith says, 'Res ipsa loquitur?'. There is no answer and after a brief pause, Sopwith responds, 'There you have it.' There is a gentle clapping and Mr. Oakbridge seems relieved as he returns to his seat, being patted on the back as he passes his friends.

Just as I think things couldn't get any stranger, Mr. Singh and Miss. Gwent are returned to the stage. The man's face covered by a comedy mask and the girl's a tragedy mask. Sopwith calls out, 'Compensatory!'. This call is met with enthusiasm as the crowd line up politely to the left to go up onto the stage, shaking the hand of the first and pushing and shoving the second, before helping themselves to an amount of money from the scales until it is eventually empty again. I watch in disgust and horror as the girl is soon on all fours, with the gentlemen sitting on her back as if she was a mule and pouring the dregs of their drink over her.

'How can you stomach this?' I protest to the barman. 'How can you let this madness go on and let them get away with it?'.

The barman takes my glass and cleans it and without emotion replies, 'I'm just the help'. I shake my head in disbelief, he wipes his hands on his waistcoat and continues,

'What makes you think they *are* going to get away with it madam?'.

I contemplate waiting to see if I will finally get the chance to speak with Sopwith but the decision is finally made for me. A string quartet hurriedly assemble onto the stage and begin to play, which is met with such a loud and incessant applause that at no point can the music even be heard. Believing I am soon to lose my mind if I stay in Aunt Sally's one moment longer, I quickly depart and my exit is as unnoticed as my entrance. My thoughts only being to get out my dress and heels as quickly and possible and change into something more comfortable. I pray I have no cause to ever enter (omitted) ever again.

*\* Ed: Maryanne, are you coping? Do you need some time off? We're not going to use this article.*

*MOS Archives, ref. INF9/909 (endorsed)*

*MOS Archives, ref. INF9/153 (illegal)*

# THE VISCOUNT

**Name: Viscount Alfie Sark**
**Location: Cliveden, Berkshire**
**Occupation: Proprietor of Cliveden**
**Threat level: 4**
**Article clearance: Silver**
**Case file: 68/3323/GBE**

My interview with Viscount Alfie Stark was requested by the interviewee, an unusual state of affairs and one with which I was not, and am not, entirely comfortable. The following is verbatim and I will leave my readers to make up their own minds about this extraordinary man, the new Lord of Cliveden.

**Viscount, thank you for agreeing to meet me.**

Oh none of that now, just call me Alfie, sweetheart. Welcome to Cliveden Communal Estate, in loyal obeisance of His Majesty and the Ministry and proud trade partners of the John Bull Co-operative Society.

**Could you explain some of your background?**

I had a pretty standard upbringing really, nothing out of the ordinary. My ma and pa were good enough folks in their own way. We grew up in Reading where my old man worked in the steel factory. My brothers and sisters mainly kept out of trouble. As for me? I was a big reader believe it or not, I loved big, epic stories. You know, the sort of adventures that a boy dreams of, cowboys and Indians, fighting the fuzzy-wuzzies, exploring lost islands. That's how I ended up in the merchant navy. A nice little life it was, not quite what I'd read in my books, but I did have a few adventures in my own way. My ship was my home. Old Sally we called the girl, and the crew were the best, roughest gentleman you'd ever know that I sailed with. See this tattoo – **It is of a fish wrapped around an anchor, done by a blind tattooist in the dark, if I am any judge** – I got that in Singapore would you believe. I've got a few more but I'd have to be naked to show you, so maybe later, only pulling your leg sweetheart!

**What were your experiences of the war?**

We were shafted, as simple as that; my ship was commandeered by the Government and we were forced to go where and when they sent us, our unarmed ship. We were making a crossing across the Atlantic and we got it from a U-boat. I don't want to forget it, but I don't want to remember it either. All my mates got it, it doesn't matter if you can swim like Esther Williams, you can't beat the ocean. Terrifying it is, you wouldn't believe, you would never understand and the cold, the icy cold, that freezes you up like a statue. I still have nightmares. I won't ever go to sea again, the bitch spared me once in her pity.

**How were you rescued?**

It was the U-boat itself, it'd come to the surface, there were a few dozen of us I suppose. I can't say I'm grateful, they were the ones that sunk us, but nothing makes sense in war, and Jerry did his best. Hours must have passed and then a bomber appeared in the sky, it was one of ours I think, and it began firing on the U-boat; everyone was waving frantically, couldn't they see the deck was full of us. I was able to get below, only a handful managed it before they closed the hatch and dived to avoid the bomber, condemning everyone on deck to death. Could you imagine the horror of that? Being rescued only to drown again? I could forgive Jerry, even if I didn't like him, it was war, but for our own men to attack us, and these weren't even fighting men remember. No, no I never forgot that.

**How were you able to return to Britain?**

That doesn't matter. It took the best part of three years, and every day was as long as a life-time. Here, what do you think of these cigarette cards? This one's a cricketer, here's a boy scout, a strong man, a ventriloquist's dummy, I designed these. See, I'm something of an entrepreneur now, these are the cigarette cards for Cliveden cigarettes. We grow the tobacco here, with a little trial and error, would you believe. You see on the edge, each one says Remember Old Sally, that's my little tribute to my mates and a little order for myself. Oh, it's a small operation of course, but I've a few trade deals going on and it's a start. I'll be honest, the cigarettes are a load of crap, we're still learning and I don't think we cure the leaves long enough but you'll smoke anything if you need it won't you?

**Why did you come to Cliveden?**

The country was in a strange place when I got back, I couldn't believe what was going on. I didn't know what to do. All I'd known was the sea, but I never wanted to go back again. Not that it mattered by then of course, there were no jobs. I made it back to Reading, but the place was in ruins, my ma and pa's house was flattened, and those that were left had no idea what had happened to them. I scraped a living for a while doing odd jobs and eventually I ran into my old mate, Harold, from when I was a nipper. He told me he was off to Cliveden, to join the Land Army, the Viscount had a communal farm of sorts, I suppose, a promise of work, a meal and a roof over your head. It was better than Reading so I went with him.

It all seemed alright at first, I suppose, we got there and were 'processed'; that was the word they used, I remember. The whole estate had turned into some sort of farm, like something from the dark ages, I reckon, peasants scattered about doing their bit. Me and Harold were put to work on the lower fields and it was back-breaking work. I didn't mind that too much, it kept me busy, but the conditions! Oh, the conditions we were under you wouldn't believe. The Viscount had fellas, and I'm not pulling your leg here, who would beat people they didn't think were working hard enough. It was barbaric, anyone who spoke up met the same fate. If we didn't like it, we could go we were told, but we all knew there was nowhere else to go, we were nothing better than slaves. We were put on rations, just enough food to keep our strength up to go to work. Here we were, hundreds of us, surrounded by food and we were all starving. The punishment for those sneaking food, well, you'd think we were slaves on some plantation. One man, and I can still picture it in my mind's eye, was lynched for sneaking cheese back to the quarters. Eventually, this sort of punishment became more common and people stopped noticing after a while.

It was all very confusing for people, and it would be wrong to judge people for tolerating it, mind. What choice did people have? Most men had wives and kids, what were they meant to do? People would tolerate anything for their families, I know that now. Me and Harold, and a few dozen of the other men, we were lucky in a way, we were single men. We didn't have to look out for anyone else, we could take risks, chances that men with families can't.

I'd never seen the Viscount or his family, but I couldn't believe they didn't condone or were even ignorant of the horrors at Cliveden, none of us could. Starvation, daily humiliation, beatings, lynchings, no, no one should have to endure that. We began talking, in secret, those we knew had nothing to lose, and we knew we had to do something and we knew, we knew we were going to kill the Viscount and his men or die trying. I'm not proud of that, but you don't know what we were suffering.

**Can you explain how the uprising started?**

I wish I could tell you it was some heroic rally, with big flags and noble men storming the gates to the cheers of the women and children, but it was nothing like that, it just happened. I remember the day before, being forced to watch as Harold got lashed for back-chatting one of the guards, his back was ripped to shreds, it was inhumane but do you know what was the final straw for me? Silly, really, I suppose, but it was a three-year-old little kid playing in the fields while his mother worked, a guard walked passed and grab him by the back of the neck and threw him violently to the ground. The mother wept, the guards laughed, but it was the boy's face. He bawled and looked at me, the guards told the mother to keep her brat on a leash. But the boy, he just looked at *me* with uncomprehending eyes, why had that happened? What did he do wrong? And do you know what I felt, I felt ashamed, and I remember, believe it or not, hunching over, and sobbing to myself, clawing the dirt with my fists, my eyes red and blinded with tears, the injustice of it all. And just like that it happened, with no thought, I got up and shouted at the guard and demanded he apologise, the guard laughed at me and went to swing at me, I blocked it and got him clear in the chin and knocked him out. I then took his lash and beat him, beat him for all my life; he stopped moving after a while. The other guards came running over to deal with me, and Harold impaled one of them with his pitchfork, one of the other lads took a scythe to another guard's neck, half hanging off his head was, half gurgling until another scythe blow to his back ended all that and then it, it just erupted. Those men who were involved, probably about thirty of us, just fought, we fought our away through the guards, through the grounds, into the estate itself, until we got to the Viscount who was with his family. His family cried and pleaded but we were deaf to it, we took him up to a window on the top floor, threw a rope around his neck, and hanged him. Then, there was nothing, no cheers of applause, no cries of protestation, no guards coming to storm us, just quiet, and the workers looking up at the window in curiosity.

We weren't monsters though, we let his wife and kids go with their servants and whatever they could carry. We did in the rest of the guards who we rounded up and we ordered everyone to the steps of the estate. We explained what had happened, those who wanted no part of it could go with no reprisals, some did and we let them go as we promised. Those who stayed would be welcome, most did. Me and the fighting lads drank that night, did we drink! We were like hooligans, smashing windows and statues, throwing paintings and books onto the fire, parading in fancy clothes; that was a night I'll never forget. The next day, when we had calmed down, we started talking about what we were going to do but, truth be told, everything was already in place, we'd just taken the figurehead and hanged him. The lads talked, and it was agreed that I should be the new Viscount for now, but it wouldn't be like before. The fighting lads all moved into the estate too and became my barons and we decided it'd be put to another vote in a years' time for who would be the new viscount.

**Was there no repercussion?**

That's the most bizarre thing, there were none, not really. We had a load of coppers turn up at the Estate once, we fought them with petrol bombs and hand to hand, it was glorious. Me and the Barons were like Bowie and his lot at The Alamo, except we won. The workers stayed out of it, but soon we had a nice set of custodian helmets to add to the collection. After we dealt with them after that – nothing, except one thing. We had some bloke in a bowler-hat and suit turn up in his car and tell us he was from The Ministry. He spurted out some nonsense and told us if we pledged allegiance to His Majesty and supplied a percentage of our crop to them, they would officially recognise the change in leadership at 'Clliveden. Of course we agreed, I don't think either us or the Ministry had the stomach for a scrap, and they probably wanted Cliveden to be in order so there we were. I was now Viscount Alfie Sark! I suppose I don't really belong in the world of privilege, but then again who does?

## How do you feel about all the pain and suffering you've experienced?

The thing about life is, it's a load of bollocks ain't it? You can try to find meaning to it; your nippers, your job, your partner, but it doesn't mean anything, except in your head.

No, no, life doesn't mean a thing and what you do won't be remembered for long. That's why there's a time limit on gravestones ain't it? You get through this life and cling on to whatever symbols and causes you like if it gets you through the day, but no one cares. Nothing you do matters, which I'm sure is a great disappointment to those who've wrapped themselves in illusion, but an absolute blessing to those to those who ain't. The lower down the ladder you are the less you have to fear.

That's why suicide rates increase the older you get, time ain't a healer, it's a cruel, viscous bastard who peels away all the layers of illusion you've made for yourself.

When you think about it, that's what's so pure and good about it all, death is the great equaliser. We all entered this world bloodied and screaming, we all leave this world on equal terms too, everything in between is just a bit of a laugh.

Try not to be scared though, death is easy, it's just like having a kip at the end of a long and bizarre day. The more tired you are, the more you appreciate it.

## How has the situation improved since your uprising?

It's clear ain't it? Look at me, I live like a king now, I drink and smoke, have my choice of the girls, wear the finest suits and have servants and everything. As long as my Barons are kept in booze and women they're all happy as a pig in mud. Cliveden cigarettes, my little pet project has been going from strength to strength, and I have quite a lucrative deal with the John Bull Co-operative Society now.

**How has the situation improved for your workers?**

Oh, the Barons keep them under control. Some of them get a bit too big for their boots sometimes and we have to deal with them, to keep the peace you know? But I think they're happy with our glorious revolution, and if they're not, then they should be.

**Do you think it would be unfair to say that nothing has changed for the people who you rebelled for?**

Well, I don't know. Remember Old Sally, that's what you get for keeping your head down and your nose clean in this life I'm afraid. Anyway, I'm much more attractive than the old Viscount, so at least there is that. Would you care for a cigarette darling?

**What do you think young Alfie, the day-dreaming bookworm of the merchant navy would think of Viscount Sark?**

I think, I think young Alfie, and his world, died with his mates the day that Old Sally was sunk.

**Alfie Stark was in tears by the end of this interview, but whether they were real or those of the reptile he really is just under the skin, is anyone's guess. Cliveden is certainly a lovely setting and who wouldn't want to be lord of all they survey? But as for an improvement in the lot of the workers – as always, regular reader, it is up to you to decide. And perhaps add Alfie Stark and**

**his myrmidons to the list of people to check should
any harm come to me or mine.**

# BRITISHERS:
# SMOKE CLIVEDEN CIGARETTES
# THE PATRIOTIC CIGARETTE

## 100% BRITISH

# THE BEST SMOKE THIS SIDE OF
# THE ATLANTIC

# THE INMATE

(Picture omitted)

Name: **Elaine Barham**
Location: **His Majesty's Prison Holloway,**
**London**
Occupation: **Convicted criminal**
Threat level: **4**
Article clearance: **Silver**
Case file: **78/7484/GBW**

NOTE: THIS IS AN UNEDITED AND
UNAPPROVED ARTICLE

I would earnestly say that the following interview
must top the list of the most bizarre I have done.
However, as my regular readers will know, with
the way things are going I dare say it won't be for
long. The source of, and reason for this interview
remains muddled. In fact, my editor seems to be
confused as to how it came about, or why I was
allowed to interview them at all, which I hope will
make sense as you read on. However, I felt it best
to go ahead, here are the notes from the interview
below and I will allow my editor to decide what is
to be done with them.

The subject of my interview is Elaine Barham,
an inmate at HMP Holloway with a string of
convictions. The women's prison is a gloomy,
huge and imposing building from the Victorian
era. After a mountain of paperwork, I was allowed
in and escorted by three wardens. The conditions
inside are close to anarchic and the prison is old,
rat-infested and overcrowded due to the sheer
number of women who have found themselves
languishing inside in recent years at His Majesty's

pleasure and as a result of the introduction of the staggering number of new laws. There appears to be some sort of organised chaos as warden's frantically struggle to keep on top of the situation though how organised it actually is would be anyone's guess.

I am lead by wardens through an unending series of metal doors, the sheer number of key's jangling from their belts and knowing which went where must be a full time job in itself. I do not wish to upset my regular readers and put them off their afternoon tea by explaining what sights, sounds and smells I experienced, but it is something which will stay with me forever I fear.

The situation became increasingly odd as the wardens insisted on showing me their star attraction before allowing me to speak to Mrs Barham. This 'attraction' was a clairvoyant within an old and disused part of the building, which was eerily silent as all but the last cell was unoccupied. The cell was cluttered with an assortment of items including an alarming amount of mirrors on the wall, a table with a crystal ball, a Ouija board, the small amount of light in the cell was concealed by black cloth hanging over the window and I was overpowered by the smell of incense. I was asked to take a seat and the wardens left. After a minute or so, I heard the sound of clinking china as an elderly and unassuming woman arrived with a tray of tea.

Tea dear?

**Thank you, what is this place?**

This dear is my home for the time. I am a clairvoyant you see, a scryer. Penny, Penny Dreadful, quite a silly name isn't it but it has a ring to it.

**Quite an impressive set up.**

Oh not really, tools of the trade and a few trinkets, the rest is just for the pantomime of it all. It's not a psychomanteum dear, funny word that isn't it? Psychomanteum.

**With the greatest respect, I'm here to visit a Mrs Elaine Barham and don't really see what this is about.**

Now, now. The wardens are quite proud to have me here and they were keen for you to meet me first so let's indulge them. I'll answer your questions shortly. May I take your hand? **(I offer my hands to Penny and am astonished how cold hers are, she turns mine over to look and my palms and pauses for a moment).**

No… no… not the Ouija board dear. Not the mirrors. The cards. Yes, the cards. Tarot cards. Please, pick one, and turn it face up onto the table.

**The hanged man? That sounds ominous.**

Oh no dear, not at all. The hanged man is to let go, to end the struggle and understand what is important. To see things from a different angle and to put your own conflict aside. This doesn't mean to stop caring dear, but simply to see that it is only you who suffers. See, look at the picture, he's hanging from the tree by his own volition. Good, pick another.

**The Hermit?**

Ah, well, that is fine. The hermit is a mysterious fellow dear. He is wise beyond understanding, but, those searching for knowledge must take great care that they do indeed really want to know the answers to their questions, for knowledge can be a terrible, terrible burden. The

91

hermit is alone you see, and represents inner guidance. The hermit does not answer your questions, but simply gives you the insight to see if the questions you are asking are the right ones. Right dear, pick one more and don't let your tea get cold.

**The Hierophant, that's a big word.**

Oh, oh, hold on dear. The hierophant is linked to the established order, you know, all the temporal clap trap - law, religion, accepted norms all that sort of thing. It represents institutions and their values but, but he can be a counsellor of sorts too, someone to turn to for wisdom and knowledge. I, I must confess dear I don't see how this fits in with the hermit and the hanged man. I feel a bit queer, give me a moment. **(Penny takes a minute or so to compose herself, dipping a biscuit into her tea before re-joining the conversation)**. So, anything you'd like to ask me?

**Yes, actually. Why are you working from a prison?**

This is as safe place as any, the top boys took a great interest in my work and they were quite insistent I come here, bless their hearts. I just need somewhere to work from, a roof over my head and a nice pot of tea. The staff treat me well and it's nice to be in the thick of it all and see what's going on. I enjoy the company, nice to be a companion for some of the girls.

**Do you not feel in danger?**

Oh no dear, the wardens are usually a good sort. Those who aren't, well, there's no paperwork for that, but I suspect they'll get their comeuppance sooner or later.

**From the inmates I meant**

No, not danger in the way I think you're suggesting dear. There is a lot of sickness here, a lot of anger and sadness, tragic really. A lot of horror. Little of it is unforgiveable though, and I've no part in all that, I'm too long in the tooth to have the audacity to judge a soul anyway. Wrong time, wrong place, wrong man mainly.

It echoes you know, tragedy echoes, somehow. The stories this old building could tell you. Though I *do* understand a lot of these ladies simply can't be out there on the streets. However, being locked in their cells from 4:30pm without food or company and living on the rations they do, it's not good for them and there aren't too many with the energy or will to kick up much of a fuss now.

I know this must sound bizarre to your ears dear, and I understand, I truly do; but there are some prayers, some laments, that are so meaningful and sincere, that one of the good chaps *has* to hear it. Don't be thrown off though, evil will always be inherently stronger than good, by its very nature, but that doesn't mean the good chaps won't roll up their sleeves and do their best, and sometimes I suspect they win too.

I do readings for the girls when the wardens allow it. Scrying, cards, Ouija, mirrors and so forth. A lot of pain dear, I can't manage too many at a time, it really does take it out of you, knocks your socks off, you see? I have to be quite selective with what I tell the girls, they've got enough on their plates and if it's something they are powerless to change or stop, I don't see the use in telling them so. A little dishonest, but it's the lesser evil I suspect dear. It's not just the girls either, I entertain the wardens, the Governor, even some of the chaps from the Ministry. There is a lot of ugliness and sadness from them too. A good deal of them belong to some very odd clubs, let me tell you. So, to answers your question in a roundabout way, the danger *I* fear, it makes no difference what side of the walls I'm on. There are some things that bricks and mortar can't keep out or in.

**If it's not a strange statement, you look, well normal. I would expect a gypsy with bangles and a head-scarf.**

Would you dear?

**What can you tell me about Mrs Barham?**

Hers is a sad story dear. She's been here many years. No one is really certain why she is in here, it's all muddled and confused, lots of conflicting accounts that she doesn't talk about, she doesn't talk much at all anymore. From what I can gather she had information, information the Ministry weren't particularly keen on her knowing, or sharing. She wasn't the sort to have any reverence for ranks and titles, not afraid to speak her mind or stand up to bullies and give them a taste of their own medicine. No dear, she seems to have riled up a few fellows with the things she knows. Best to make an example of her, get her out of the way I think. Oh, Elaine Barham is no saint, ruffled a few feathers, but she shouldn't be here. It's a queer analogy, but the Ministry lot do baffle me; they're like a child furiously guarding a sand-castle they've proudly made. No, ignore me I'm rambling. Anyway, some of the innocent girls are driven mad with anger or despair at the injustice of it all. Waste of energy though really isn't it? I'd dare say Elaine has been very stoic and restrained in the circumstances.

**I have read a few articles in the papers about Elaine, but they're a bit vague and convoluted and don't really give much a way.**

Yes, I wouldn't read that nonsense dear.

**Why doesn't she talk about it? Surely something can be done.**

That's very sweet dear, nothing can be done. She'd drive herself mad if she kept dwelling on what had happened to her. Her story isn't as uncommon as you'd think anyway. If she spoke out, it'd be nothing but trouble for those closest to her. There's no one who has the ability, appetite or inclination to help her, there's no one who can fix things. Not here anyway.

**If I may say without causing offence. I'm not really sure why I am here, not just with you but in this prison at all. My editor doesn't even seem to be sure who invited me.**

I wouldn't concern yourself with that sort of thing dear.

**May I ask, have you had any experience with Mr. Ravenley the magician, given what you do?**

**(Penny appears to begin speaking, but then gazes off into the bottom of her cup for a moment before continuing).** He's not someone I'm really interested in dear. My work isn't particularly complimentary to his. We're not really after the same things. You're an interesting one though, would you mind if I had a look at your future?

**How?**

Through my crystal ball dear. Won't be a moment. **(Penny places her hand around the ball and stares into it without emotion).** Have you finished your tea dear?

*What did you see?*

Oh nothing dear, not to worry. **(Penny takes my cup and studies the tea leaves at the bottom and appears to frown).** You're not one for all this superstitious nonsense are you? It's fine, you can be honest, it won't hurt my feelings.

**I'm afraid I don't believe in any of it.**

I don't blame you, with all these charlatans and frauds about. I don't know why people who think they have talents feel the need to shout it from the roof tops. Really does give the business a bad name dear. The way I see it, people should see they are playing with the emotions of desperate souls, it's not a game and some things probably shouldn't be known. (**Penny taps her fingers on the crystal ball and puts a cloth over it**). I think we're done now, take care won't you? I wish you all the best, sincerely.

**Thank you Penny.**

My pleasure dear, don't be a stranger.

**I left the unlocked cell to find the three wardens waiting at the far end. The odd serenity of Penny's room disappeared as I came crashing back to reality and the appalling conditions of the prison. After a few minutes of being navigated through the chaos, I realised I wasn't being taken to another wing, I was being returned to the entrance. Through the cries, the moans and the sobbing I could just about make out what the wardens were saying to me. There were a few more forms to sign before leaving.**

**I must confess, I was absolutely relieved to be out of there, the air never felt so fresh as I left the husk of HMP Holloway and the bright blue sky, the grass and the trees felt strange for a few moments. The insane and oppressive raucousness of the building was now replaced with the gentle singing of swallows. I was led by one warden off the grounds. I cannot fathom why Penny Dreadful**

is inside that building, as it is clearly causing her some distress, but she appears to know what she is doing and there are some things in this world I feel it's best to let be. Penny Dreadful's story is one sleeping dog I feel I should not disturb.

The day came to nightmarish grand finale when I asked the warden why I had been taken off site before meeting Elaine Barham, as per my interview request. The warden simply replied, 'You did. Penny Dreadful *is* Elaine Barham. She's a witch, don't you know?'.

I'm trying not to dwell on the absurdity of a witch inside a prison or the reasons why. After realising that somehow *the tower* tarot card ended up in my notebook, my regular readers may sympathise that my first stop after HMP Holloway was for a stiff gin and tonic.

*(Editor: This interview makes me feel a bit uneasy. Unless we work out where our invitation came from, my gut feeling is not to pursue this one any further and leave it out of publication).*

Mr. Arnold, a known criminal, gave a detailed account of what had lead him to contact ███████. He did not take the situation seriously and appeared to find it amusing. He rambled about delusional stories of ████████████ and and claimed that his earlier arrest by ████████ was an ████████████████, ████████ and act an of ████████████ .

Mr. Arnold is clearly very clever and well aware of the offences he has committed but disturbingly expresses no remorse for them.

He has been provided bail on the condition that he does not contact any ███████████████████████████████ , particularly his victim, ███████ .

When questioned if Mr. Arnold posed a risk to children, he became extremely ███████ and ███████ , most likely an admission of guilt.

Police Constable PUGH

(FORWARDED TO PROSECUTION)

# THE POLICEMAN

**Name: Bill Dixon**
**Location: Bidford-on-Avon**
**Occupation: Police Officer (retired)**
**Threat level: 3**
**Article clearance: Silver**
**Case file: 12/2999/GBL**

I was fortunate to be able to interview ex-police officer Dixon, as most people who have held official positions are excluded from all contact with any press or media of any description. However, through some administrative glitch, all too common these days but often working in the favour of the wrong (or in this case, right) person, I was granted permission and the interview below is the result. Excuse in advance, regular reader, the rather pedantic content; Mr Dixon seems unable to just 'go' somewhere, without proceeding in a northerly (or whichever is appropriate) direction. I have tried my best to weed out his more byzantine sentences; with how much success, you must be my judge.

Thank you for speaking to me, Mr Dixon.

My pleasure, call me Bill. Old Bill actually. Due to my age that was my nickname. I always wanted to be a policeman since I was a boy, like my father before me, so I was delighted when I was accepted into Warwickshire and Coventry Constabulary. Luckily I had the height, and the moustache to pull it off!

What was it like being a policeman in the early days?

It was a bloody nightmare, thank you for asking. When war broke out, all the Borstal boys who'd served six months were released, along with any inmate up and down the country who only had three months or less to serve on their sentences. The chaps at the station weren't pleased with that, no, not pleased at all. The war thinned our ranks considerably, believe it or not, down some fifty percent, I believe it was, within very few months. We tried to play it down, but the villains soon cottoned on to the fact. Jewellery, that was one of the big ones, robbing jewellers, having the bottle to do it in the cold light of day so confident were they. We were kept busy morning, noon and night, though I won't lie to you, the overtime came in handy. Our wives got used to not seeing us too often and there were those who in the end decided they didn't want to see us at all. Oh, yes, very high separation rate there was in the Force in those early years. Course, I was already too old for that kind of shenanigans. My wife, she'd shut up shop in that respect years before, so no loss to me. But yes, the overtime came in handy.

The main headache, as I'm sure you can guess, was bombings and blackouts. Criminals loved a blackout, you can use your imagination to guess what sort of things they could get away with in pitch black. If we were lucky, it was a gangster using it to get revenge on one of his ilk, if not, it was some innocent. It's one thing to be able to tell the difference between the bombs and a murder when the smoke clears, it's another to be able to deal with it.

When the air raid sirens went, that meant two things. First, obviously that bombs were probably coming our way and second, the thieves would be out. The villains loved that sound, it meant the streets would be empty. I remember one time, and we never caught him, there was one lad, with an ARP armband and helmet who was smashed his way into a store and was loading up a van as bombs were falling only a mile or so away and the air was thick with smoke. The funniest thing, and I suppose I have to admire him in his way, he'd even convinced a couple to help him load up the van, must have told them he was taking the goods for safekeeping or some nonsense. He drove off before I could get to him.

Another time, and you'll have to forgive me for this, I remember a butcher's shop taking a direct hit, people were in there. The scum was rummaging around stealing the meat, but, it wasn't always clear to me what was meat and what was, you know, human remains.

Coupons, the blaggards loved coupons, clothing coupons, petrol coupons. They'd get their hands on these in any way they could, trading them for people who had no use for their cars, back-handers from dodgy shopkeepers, even taking them right from the warehouses. And spivs, don't get me started on them, pencil-moustaches, pin-striped suits, trilby hats. Absolute cads and womanisers, suitcases bulging with stockings, sugar, saucy pictures, tobacco, alcohol. All 'fallen off the back of a lorry' of course.

**Did you and your colleagues feel able to cope with this new crime?**

It became very difficult, as a policeman, even if we'd never say it; you need to know when to deal with something and when to turn a blind eye. People looting shops hit by the bombs, mixed with, and often the same people clearing the rubble, was one of them. Firemen were terrible for it, I remember a house on fire and the firemen were climbing down the ladder, singing their hearts out, wearing fur coats and jewellery over their uniforms, the men holding the ladders laughing their heads off. We'd look away with things like that. Due to the alcohol shortage, people were brewing 'Hooch', god that'd blow your socks off and you could tell when someone had had a snifter of that, but drunkards more often than not, weren't worth the time.

Stealing wallets, purses, wedding rings straight from the dead, that was the worst, something I could never stomach and you can believe me when I tell you we'd deal with those we caught doing that in the manner it deserved. Business owners dreaded the air-raid sirens, knowing the villains would do more damage than the bombs often did. Shop windows covered in plywood and boarded up only took moments for a seasoned robber to get past.

**How widespread do you think corruption was?**

Corruption was everywhere, few people came out of all that clean, I'm afraid. Even doctors, yes that's right doctors, they'd sign people off, for a price, for those who didn't want to be called up, forging certificates, diagnosing wounds and illnesses that weren't there and there was simply too much chaos and anarchy to deal with all that, all the time. And the thing about corruption is, when one person sees another get away and profit from corruption without repercussion, it encourages them to do the same.

Genuine businessmen, with contracts with the government, they'd fiddle their books, make out they were employing people who didn't exist or didn't work for them just to get their pay packets, sharing it with their ghost-workers who were real, pocketing it themselves for those who weren't. Our children, who were evacuated to the countryside, the families that took them in were even guilty. Claiming billets for children that didn't exist!

The government would compensate those who had their homes bombed by the Luftwaffe, one cheeky sod claimed his home had been bombed a dozen times! We nicked him, but others were doing it all the time and the Government was drowning under paperwork working out who was genuine and who wasn't.

**How did this affect you personally? Did you think these criminals were evil?**

Did it affect me? Yes, yes, it's fair to say I lost a lot of faith in people in those days, can I blame them? No, not at all, but it doesn't make it right.

The trouble with evil, and good, is that they are absolutes. Life doesn't work like that. We are all of us good and evil in our own ways, they aren't permanent homes, it is a sliding scale each of us moves up and down every day, based on our actions. A youngster poaching or stealing some bread for his siblings, he's a criminal isn't he? A man murdering his wife in cold blood of course is a criminal too. A policeman battering a lad to death for a crime he wasn't even sure he committed, he's a criminal. Everyone has a different angle of looking at it, a different cut-off point. You've got to remember, and it took me a long time to learn this, the police, the police courts, they're not about justice, they're about order. They are two very different things. Justice is a dream, an ideal, there's too much injustice I've seen to be convinced otherwise. Order, that's easier, punishing people for crimes, keeping discipline, and if a few innocent people get caught up in that, well, their voices are soon drowned out.

## Do you think the police's integrity was affected?

Oh yes, without a doubt, in every sense. There was a lot of frustration at the station. I remember one young officer telling the Sergeant a young girl had reported being raped. He was very angry, very frustrated with all that was happening, his face was bright red and he slammed his fist on the lad's desk, 'Bloody nick her,' he screamed. So we did, there she was, a young girl who was raped was arrested and accused of making it up and wasting police time, 'This is what happens we you lie,' we said. Think she tried to kill herself in the end. The Sergeant and the chiefs didn't seem to care who was getting nicked and convicted, and on what grounds, as long as someone was getting their collar felt. Once these poor sods were in front of the magistrates they were easy pickings, they didn't have a chance against the Police Inspectors.

We covered up for each other. At the time I thought it was a force for good, but I realised how wrong we were, there was one officer who was a womaniser and an adulterer, sleeping with wives whose husbands were off fighting. Well, one day, the husband came home unexpectedly and the officer jumped from a second storey window and broke his leg. We made out he injured himself chasing down the husband who was mugging a neighbour, he got a pasting. I remember one time, someone had made a complaint about one of the officers and, as you can imagine, we don't look favourably on those who complain about us. He was protesting that he'd been treated unjustly, his earlier arrest was unlawful and his interview was biased and abusive. Do you know what we did? We went through his complaint with a fine-tooth comb, looking for anything to nick him for, and we did. We nicked him for harassment of a police officer, we locked him up in custody without food or drink, freezing his arse off in the cell. That, well, that was the first time I was ashamed. I don't pretend to be a saint, policemen will always look out for each other, 'Don't let the truth get in the way of a good prosecution'; 'Always choose loyalty over honesty'; and 'Turkeys don't vote for Christmas'; I knew the game. But when I saw that chap, stunned and confused, being lead into custody, clearly no idea what he was doing there, simply for complaining, as was his right, about a police officer. When he was in his cell, they blasted 'The Laughing Policeman' into his cell over and over. It wasn't only immoral, it was inhuman. That was the first time I took a step back, and knew we'd gone too far.

**How did things change for you?**

After that, my mind became clearer, I was acutely aware of everything we were doing wrong, but what could I do about it? Being a copper and complaining about your own is a death sentence, trust me. I remember seeing some graffiti on a ruined building saying 'The Old Bill are not your friends! Say nothing!' and I realised this is what a substantial number of people thought of us. You see, being a policeman is to be an actor really, you have to believe it, and your audience have to believe it, if either of those parts breaks down then the whole facade comes crashing down.

We weren't above the law, we *were* the law, and if anyone dared speak out or complain, well, we were the ones who dealt with those complaints, and why on earth would we give attention to anyone that was going to condemn our own?

The way people were treated by us, well, it was on a coin toss really, if we couldn't be bothered then you'd be fine. If we'd had a bad day or wanted to take our frustrations out on anyone, then, well, we were judge and jury. If we wanted to nick someone, we would, it's easy, too easy. You just need to poke, prod and antagonise them until they do or say something you can lift them for, it's just a matter of time. We had a journalist once, who spoke up against the Constabulary, we brought him into the station for 'an informal chat', made him didn't think he needed a solicitor. Kept chipping, chipping away it him, 'You're obviously very clever and good at hiding your tracks, we're very disturbed you have access to children' we said. That riled him, when he challenged us, well, we had him for harassment of a police officer and you can get away with treating criminals like second class citizens. I remember a group of young lads on a street corner who matched the description of some shoplifters, we went up to them and gave them all a thump. One of the lads tried to fight back, so, with assault of a police officer now committed, we beat him with our truncheons. Do you know what our nickname became among the young lads? The Black and Blues, quite imaginative really, because that was the state anyone we didn't take a liking to ended up. Being a policeman, particularly through what Coventry was suffering, should have been about fair play rather than the technicalities of breaching the peace and the desire to feel collars. One officer could give a man a verbal warning, and if another officer didn't like the look of him, he'd go back the next day and nick him anyway. We lost a lot of respect in the community, and I cannot blame them for it.

As the situation in Coventry got worse, and order was breaking down, we were given more and more rule to apply the law as we saw fit and, well, we fell. We lost all our moral fibre. We became more like an armed gang than anything else. Corruption amongst the police was ignored and seen as acceptable in the circumstances. There was once thirty or so of us scrapping in the streets with a gang of about twenty lads and I remember thinking 'What is going on?' Had we backed these lads into a corner so much, made them so desperate, did they despise us so much that they were willing to brawl in the street with us like we were a common street gang? I remember one of my colleagues laughing afterwards, patting me on the back and saying 'Nice bit of overtime there.'

Often I'd see people being taken off in the back of a police van, not sure the usual sort, but women and children too. I'd ask where they were going, 'Don't concern yourself,' was the Sergeant's response.

I started to despise myself and the uniform I was wearing. Where once I was delighted to see a bobby, it suddenly became very oppressive, like my chest was caving in, and I was one of them, heaven forbid what others thought of us. But the truth is, people believed, or wanted to believe we were the good guys, of course they would, people don't want to think of the bobby on the beat being a bad apple. People will believe what they want to believe, if they want to believe someone is good they will, if they want to believe someone is wicked they will, and they will ignore anything that goes against that. Do you know what I can't stand the sound of now? Police whistles; stupid isn't? But they fill me with dread now.

**What happened to you?**

It was an absolutely stupid thing to do, but I tried having a quiet word with the Inspector, just to explain my thoughts and concerns, let him know what people thought of us. He seemed to take it all in and thanked me. The next day, it was announced that due to my age and the circumstances I was being dismissed. Because of my long-service I would receive a pension and they would 'overlook any indiscretions', but that was it, there was something that tried to imitate a leaving party, and then I was gone. I did try to stay in touch with a lot of them as they were my friends, but I was given a quite word that I was considered a pariah now, and my old colleagues had been advised not to have any contact with me as I was a 'potential reputational risk', I believe is how it was worded.

The years passed and when Coventry ended, so did the police force, and my pension. Now I scrape a living with my family here, it's a hard life but at least it's honest and, well, as long as I never hear another police whistle as long as I live, then I'll be grateful. The police that exist this day, they're a different breed to me. There are even the Blue Lampers the so-called vigilantes who seem to be constantly scrapping with the bobbies, keeping them in check. But really they're all cut from the same cloth and as bad as each.

**Bill, you may be aware, there are those within the Constabulary that claim it was in fact you who was the corrupt one, which is why you were dismissed. How do you respond to that?**

I can't take on an entire Constabulary, no one can, it is insurmountable. Remember the role of the police is fluid, flexible. As long as you tick the boxes and 'satisfy the process', then anything is possible.

**Do you still believe in justice?**

I agree that justice is blind, and probably deaf and dumb too and her scales are well off kilter. Other than that, the less said the better.

We need to get ██████████████, keep ██████, ████████████████ you can at him. If he's not ████████. ████████████ at his house or something, use your initiative. I'm not going to have the ██████ of my officers questioned like that, ████████ ████████ think he is.
Go through his ██████, find someone he has ██████████ during his career, get them to ████████. ████ him to ████████. Keep ████████, we'll get something on this ████, ████████████. I want this man in a ████ by the end of the ████.

Police Inspector PUGH

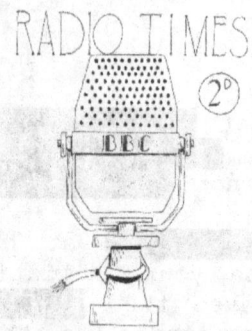

**Witford Radio - 1570kHz MW**
*Putting the spunk back in Blighty*

Lupino Lane - The Lambeth Walk

Jack Judge - It's A Long Way To Tipperary

LISTING OF ENEMIES OF HIS MAJESTY

George Formby - Andy The Handy Man

Marie Lloyd - Every Little Movement Has A
Meaning Of Its Own

THE KING'S SPEECH

Leslie Sarony - Jollity Farm

Flanagan and Allen - Run Rabbit Run

DEMILITARISED ZONES UPDATE

Henry Hall & His Orchestra - The Teddy
Bear's Picnic

Flanagan and Allen - Maybe It's Because I'm A Londoner

THE LORD WIND-BAG SHOW

Florrie Forde - Hold your hand out, Naughty Boy

The Two Leslies - In the Land of Inky Pinky Dinky Doo

*MOS Archives, ref. INF9/636 (endorsed)*

# THE STARLET

**Name: Dame Joan 'Miss Mauve' Creighton-Ward**
**Location: King's Manor, York**
**Occupation: Chairwoman of the John Bull Co-operative Society/Singer**
**Threat level: 2**
**Article clearance: Silver**
**Case file: 55/2935/GBW**

I went to see Dame Joan on a blustery day; my plans to take a stroll in her garden was not welcomed because the wind would tousle her hair. Older readers will doubtless remember Miss Mauve's few performances with such greats as Buster Keaton and Charlie Chaplin but younger readers may need to consult a grandparent to find out who she is. Notwithstanding, I was ushered into the presence with much ceremony and certainly it is hard to believe, when in her rather cluttered boudoir, that Dame Joan is not a living icon of cinema rather than the rather sad old lady which I found myself interviewing. She refused a photographer as she had recently had a cold; her appearance in daylight, which she avoids as far as possible, was probably not all she hoped, as the layers of white makeup, applied one on top of the other with little recourse to soap and water in between did not show off to best advantage her celebrated 'peaches and cream' complexion. But, when all is said and done, she is a game old lady, marching on regardless in a world which she may not totally understand these days. If the spotlight under which she lives with Mitzi, Daphne and Lulu

**is not as real as she imagines, it would be a cruel visitor who would tell her so.**

**Thank you for taking the time to meet me, Dame Joan.**

Oh, just call me Joan, darling. Excuse the clutter, I really should have the boys clear this out. It's a bit of a squeeze but we'll find you somewhere to sit; don't mind the dogs, they're old softies. Stop yapping, ladies, this lovely young woman is our guest. There, now, do you like the furniture? Baroque, Parisian, hand-crafted by Jean Charles. Louis! Louis! Get this girl a drink will you dear, some vol au vents, there's a dear man. (**Dame Joan treats her servant like a devoted admirer; happily for the poor old lady, her eyesight prevents her from seeing his expression, which is anything but devotion**)

**Joan, is it true you used to be an actress?**

Oh yes, a famous one at that, I was the most beautiful woman in all of the West End. My golden hair, my songbird voice, men would, and did, commit many crimes of passion for my hand. Oh what a delightful game it all was, the turn of the century, the good old days. Here, take this photo album. There's me in 'A Chinese Honeymoon', that one there, that's my first ever performance, there I am at the Empress Ladies Club too. Oh look, I'm a flapper girl in that one. Wonderful memories darling, absolutely delightful. And then film of course; only silent – I wouldn't have any truck with those talkies. They'll never catch on.

**How did you become involved in the entertainment industry?**

Well, you'd never believe it to see me now, but I used to be as common as muck, do you know. I was born into very unfortunate circumstances and a most unhappy state of domesticity; I escaped my family as soon as I could. I had nothing, nothing at all, except my beauty, and my voice. I used to sing in the pubs and was discovered by a cad named Bates. I didn't know at the time but he was a most vulgar fellow, darling. I was young, and impressionable, with stars in my eyes and I fell for his stories of fame and riches, and he became, for want of a better word, my agent.

I never made it to the West End with him though, darling; instead I became an entertainer at the Gentleman's Clubs. They were some dark days let me tell you and it was rarely my ballads they were after. You'd positively blush if you knew the sorts of things these married, respectable, powerful men desired in the night. Outright perverse, but, because of my beauty, I was treasured, and I was always in control, always calling the shots, yes, believe that, dear. But still, I did grow to hate these men, these church-going men, minsters some of them and I kept a little book, yes a little black book of those particularly villainous men who had come to my attention.

There was one chap, Mr. Brownlow, at the John Bull club, the chairman in fact, who was as queer as the rest of them but he had a softness and a kindness to him too. He wanted to take me away, 'My bird in a gilded cage' he'd call me. He knew my desires still lay in acting and singing, and he was a powerful man. He got me a few auditions and the rest is history. 'Miss Mauve' was born. Bates had been watching me at all my shows without my knowledge; once he even burst into my dressing room when I was alone to try to take me against my will. He was obsessed with me, on his knees in tears, thumping the ground, begging for my love, telling me he'd do anything for me, anything as long as he could be near me. I dealt with him and Mr. Brownlow pulled enough strings that it was never an issue, bless his heart.

**(At this point, Louis returned with drinks and vol au vents; he was clearly doing his best in straitened circumstances; the sherry was rather watered down and the vol au vents were empty**

**save for a sliver of potted meat. However, Dame Joan seemed oblivious and, raddled though she might be these days, there is something in her tarnished glory that makes it impossible to upset her.)**

Louis, be a dear; will you put 'A Bird in a Gilded Cage' on. Here darling, listen this is me, wonderful isn't it?

**(The gramophone is as old and out of touch as its owner, but the weak voice warbling through the static still holds some of the old charm. Joan mouths silently along with the words, waving a finger more or less in time with the music. A foot taps under her gauzy wrap and one of the dogs howls in sympathy.)**

**Thank you for that, performance, Joan.**

My pleasure, you lucky thing you. Where were we? Ah yes. My career went from strength to strength and Miss Mauve became a household name. I was the embodiment of the West End, and all the mystery and glamour that went with it. This picture of me here, long flowing blonde hair covering one eye, those lips, yes, this picture was everywhere. They were simply wonderful years. I married Mr. Brownlow and we lived like royalty in London.

But as always, the charm of a gentleman soon disappears, Mr. Brownlow turned out to be little better than Mr. Bates in the end. Mr. Brownlow simply didn't trust me; he knew my background, you see and he became consumed with jealousy, I really did become a bird in a gilded cage, I tell you, and he hated, absolutely hated, the thought of other men pining after me. He would never say it, but I knew he was doing everything he could behind the scenes to end my career, and he managed it. There were even rumours circulating that I had died, could you believe it! Mr. Brownlow demanded I became a mother to his children but I'd told him a thousand times, due to my time with Mr. Bates and the Gentleman's Clubs, it wasn't possible for me to be a mother. I tried to leave Mr. Brownlow, but it seemed, I was under house arrest! Every attempt to leave would end in failure, with the punishment more severe each time, so in the end I simply stopped trying.

One day, Mr. Brownlow had that unfortunate automobile accident; do you remember it? No, darling, of course you don't; you weren't even born then. Drunk as a mule he was and his estate was bequeathed to me. That's when I really began to live again. I met another chap named Mr. Pickering, who I had known from the John Bull club, not a lover mind but a friend, and my career began again. That was when I had my little flutter in the films, but the Americans were so coarse, darling, they didn't understand my art at all, so I came straight back home.

I suppose I didn't realise how many years had passed. Would you believe, darling, the first show I played was to an empty hall! I didn't mind, it was nice to have the practice and I don't think it was promoted very well. I think some people didn't even believe I was Miss Mauve as it had been so long. Still, Mr Pickering had every faith in me; I even used some of Mr. Brownlow's estate to buy a hall, which Mr Pickering ran, so I could perform every night. There was never much of an audience, but it's the quality not the quantity of the crowd that matters. And then of course, darling, war came. Louis! Louis! Would you be a dear and refill our drinks, thank you sweetie.

**(The topped up sherry was even weaker, but Dame Joan scarcely seemed to notice. I do wonder, in retrospect, whether the sherry was watered down for economy's sake, or to keep the Dame off the hard stuff for as long as possible.)**

**How did the war affect things for you?**

Not too much for me I suppose. I remember one night playing in the hall when the sirens went off and the bombs began to fall. The handful of people in the audience fled, but, well, I'm a professional, darling. I carried on with the show, despite the protests of the band. Though how on earth anyone could appreciate my contralto with all that racket is beyond me.

I remember a meeting with Mr Pickering; he told me he wanted to expand into wholesale supplies, due to the awful rationing that was taking place. He had enough friends in the John Bull club but just needed the initial investment. As the war went on, 'The John Bull Co-operative Society' was born. Oh, I know lots of people didn't approve, nothing but spivs and crooks people would say, but there was a demand, and Mr. Pickering supplied it. With their sharp looks, we brought back a bit of much needed glamour to the country and my hall, well, it was soon bustling. Miss Mauve was the talk of the town again!

**(Dame Joan's mind is not wandering, as such, but any conversation with her needs a sharp attention to detail to keep up with her. She is suddenly concerned with her clothes for an evening out.)**

Louis, Louis, would you pick me out an outfit for this evening dear, not the hat though. Thank you darling.

Where was I? Oh, yes; with the ghastly state in London, we decided to relocate to York where there was another John Bull club. I missed the old hall but the new one is just as good, if not better. With the state of the Government, people began to love the John Bull Co-operative Society, and who can blame them.

**The John Bull Co-operative Society has been accused of simply being a front for organised criminality, smuggling, extortion and racketeering, Joan. How do you respond to that?**

Oh, we've attracted the odd rogue but Mr. Pickering deals with all of that thing. For me, it's the show business. What people need right now is glitz, and Miss Mauve does glitz like nobody's business. I was made a Dame by His Majesty, so we can't be that bad, can we, sweetheart?

**Do you ever think back to your younger years?**

Of course I do, darling, but well, I'm loving every moment still. In fact, I'm performing tonight. You should come down; I'll get the boys to get you on the guest-list, I assume you don't have a plus one. Louis, be a dear and play 'After The Ball is Over' will you? I want to practice.

**(Although the look that Joan gave me when she assumed I didn't have a plus one was one of hardly veiled contempt, I confess to still having a grudging admiration for the old girl. She is oblivious to the way she is being used and in a way, where's the harm? She gets to warble the old tunes and the punters get some under the counter bacon. I think anyone who remembers the poor old soul from her heyday wouldn't wish her ill. Although, she still had a surprise up her frilly sleeve.)**

**Thank you Dame Joan; let me check my commitments and I'll try to make it. One last question, do you ever think back to how your life would be different if you never met Mr. Bates? Do you miss him, ever?**

No, no need for that. And how can I miss him? He's right here, Louis Bates, isn't that right Louis?

**I was ushered out of Dame Joan's boudoir by Louis, a sly smile on his lips and a hand on a buttock, which I shrugged off with no apology. The world today is a weird place, anyone would agree and getting weirder. This occasional series on the man and woman in the street is teaching me more than anything that you certainly can't judge a book**

**by its cover; is Dame Joan a dupe and a bit of a senile old hoofer, or is she one of the most successful black marketeers the country has yet produced. Let the reader decide!**

# THE PRIZEFIGHTER

(Picture omitted)

**Name: Tom Tiddler**
**Location: Empire Theatre, Aldershot**
**Occupation: Pugilist**
**Threat level: 1**
**Article clearance: Bronze**
**Case file: 22/9367/GBE**

NOTE: THIS IS AN UNEDITED AND
UNAPPROVED ARTICLE

The imposing Empire Theatre is still a magnificent building, and if it was not for the occasional flurry of bullet holes on the outside plaster, you'd be forgiven for thinking this former military garrison town had no involvement in earlier events.

Inside the Empire Theatre there is a din of activity, inside the main auditorium workmen appear to be reorganising chairs and setting up a boxing ring. While on the stage itself, there appears to be a rehearsal for, I assume, an am dram version of *Tristan Und Isolde* judging by the wailing of the out of key singers.

However, my interviewee today is the famous prize-fighter Tom Tiddler who is clearly something of a local hero judging by the posters of him plastered carelessly throughout the town in abandoned shop windows. Fisticuffs appears a popular past time in Aldershot as I personally witness three brawls as my made my way to the venue. I am taken to an upstairs room where I find Tom, naked I fear, except for a fig leaf covering his modesty. He is a large, broad man with a bald

**head and a moustache that would make any Victorian strongman proud. He stares at me, frozen to the spot pulling a heroic pose and the moments that follow are very odd. Fortunately, this is broken by the flash of a camera as I realise Tom is posing for a photographer. Behind the camera, a somewhat flamboyant man squeals with delight.**

*'Hercules dear! Hercules incarnate. Bravo, bravo. What a sight for sore eyes.'*

Hello love, you must be the journo, come over take a seat I won't be long.

*'Yes, yes, do take a seat. Tom dear, don't move your head stay still.'*

**(It is difficult talking to a naked Hercules, frozen like a statue, with only his eyes following me to my seat like a living Mona Lisa but I persevere.)**

**Hello Tom, I'm sorry to disturb you, it appears to be a bad time?**

No such thing as a bad time love.

**What is this photo-shoot for it I may ask?**

You know what? I have no idea, it's all part of the job though.

*'Hercules! Darling! Please keep your head still, and… oil, yes more oil, let's make those muscles sparkle!'.*

**(The situation becomes increasingly more uncomfortable as the photographer begins to liberally slather oil across Tom's body).**

**I, I think I'll come back later.**

No, no, now is fine. So, are you going to ask me any questions or just stand their gawping?

**Yes... You have a big fight tonight I believe?**

Oh yes, one of the biggest, get yourself a seat this will be one for this history books. Jack Sprat!

*'No sweetheart, that was cancelled remember. It's Peking Tom.'*

Oh, well we can't be both called Tom can we?

*'You're right, I'll speak to his people, see what we can do.'*

**Peking Tom?**

Southpaw, good reach on him though. Little fella, only 180lbs but don't be fooled, I saw him take down John Mace in two rounds. Feisty fella. Looking forward to it.

**How have current events affected your line of work?**

Not at all, probably made boxing more popular I reckon. I hear that the War has, well, made people a bit funny. Up for a risk, up for a bit of danger and violence. I think the War taught a lot of folks that life is cheap, seize the day and all that cobblers.

*'Carpe Diem!'* (**the photographer sings before repositioning himself to massage oil into Tom's thighs**).

Why not. Chaps need danger don't they? Half the fellas in this town were soldiers weren't they, trained to kill, full of anger and rage and violence, now they're doing nothing but shuffling about looking for work, nothing to do with all their talents. Asking for trouble really isn't it? If the boxing keeps their tempers under control, well, I'm doing the public a service.

**Do any of these men attempt to fight you themselves?**

Some of them get carried away in the heat of the moment, like animals in the crowd they are, getting swept away by the blood and the frenzy of it. It's exhilarating, when I'm in that ring, the crowd going bananas, oh its paradise, you feel like a God. The odd fella fancies his chance and runs into the ring, but normally the boys lamp them before they get too far. If they want to fight me they can, I'll take anyone on but they should do it the right way, work their way to the top. Go through the county leagues, up to national, then... if they survive to the Brassneck Tourney, I'll give them the bloody nose they've been hoping for.

**The Brassneck Tourney?**

The top boys, league of champions, the real men. Me; Cheeky Blighter; Potato Pete; Peking Tom; Jack Sprat; Macey; Uncle Reg; Sexton; Old Phil; Bosch; Frank Knuckles; Billy Beef... who are those two queer brothers?
*'Dandelion and Burdock!'*
Them. There's a lot of others, but we're the best stable.

**How many fights do you think you've had in your professional career?**

Seventy... seventy-five, something like that.

**You seem in remarkable condition if I may say.**

*'Doesn't he just!'*
I wouldn't be fooled; I've had my fair share. I got a lamp good and proper from Uncle Reg, and Fisticuff Franky almost made me give up in my earlier days. I've had this annoying clicking jaw ever since, absolute pain in my rump. Drives me mad. There's a little dot in my left eye too, just above my field of vision, drives me to distraction love, I keep trying to look at it but of course it moves away

when I do. You're right though, I'm more of a giver then a taker. All part of the fun though.

**How did you become involved in boxing?**

Same as most of the other lads really. I was ex-forces and, like I said earlier, it was hard suddenly being back on civvie street. We'd been changed you see, trained into killing machines and then, 'thank you, good bye and good luck', that was hard, hard for all of us. A lot of bitterness, unsettled issues, rage…

    *'Rage, rage against the dying of the light!'*

    A lot of boys turned to drink, we were reckless, care-free, sporting for violence and misadventure that would never come. Trained for something we weren't wanted for. A lot of those miserable wretches took it out on their wives and kids, not being able to cope with civvie street. Full of misery and night terrors, haunted by what they'd seen at Dunkirk, Brighton, Birmingham, all that.

    You see, boxing saved me, saved a lot of boys. Finally, we had somewhere constructive for all our energy, somewhere for our demons to live and thrive, for the rage to be fed. I took to it like a fish in water. I've always been a scrapper, did a lot in the forces, and it was an old comrade who got me involved in the county league. Brawling with the amateurs was as easy as you like, and I sailed my way up to the National League and from there, a good year or so and I was a Brassnecker, a champion, and that's where the real money is.

**Do you think you were a good soldier?**

No such thing as a good or a bad soldier love, only orders.

**Do your family worry for you?**

No, what else would I do? There is nothing else.

    *'Oh don't be so melodramatic silly.'*

Devil makes work for idle hands.

*'Mister Tom you're very close to queer. What on Earth have you been reading, Dostoyevsky?'*

Just saying, it's a touchy subject for me.

**What would you say to the more restrained factions who think you are thugs and monsters?**

Monsters? What else can we do. We are the rejected, the abandoned, the forgotten. We're not wanted or needed. The War is not over for us, not one of us, until the day we die. If we are monsters, they made us.

'Poetry, pure poetry for such a big brute.'

I've seen too many fellas disappear, whether with a rope round their necks or at the bottom of a glass. Nothing will kill a man like rejection. From his loved ones, his comrades, society; it's all the same. No, better to find a way to keep going, keep fighting. As I was taught in my squaddie days; improvise, adapt and overcome.

*'and be marvellous!'*

**Thank you for speaking to me Tom, and good luck for your fight tonight.**

Thank you love, you should come along.

*'Hold still dear!'*

**I must confess to having a slight admiration for Tom, he is certainly a pragmatic pugilist and his fellow brawlers perhaps are of the same mind. They have made the best of a bad situation. Although they are clearly full of sadness and rage; they are stoic about it and restrict their brutish activity to inside the ring, against those who want to fight them, in front of people who want to witness it, something many denizens in this country could learn a lesson or two from. Given what Tom alludes to have suffered, I would dare**

say he is particularly restrained and I struggle to picture this man fighting. I left the photographer to continue meticulously oiling my interviewee. Full of morbid curiousity, I returned to the Empire Theatre that evening and was able to purchase a ticket from a spiv to watch Tom Tiddler fight his opponent, Peking Tom (clearly the name change request was denied).

The Empire Theatre was full to capacity that evening, with the electric energy that only comes from a crowd of alcohol induced excitable men. There was a deafening roar, and an unceasing bumping of shoulders and spilled drinks as Tom entered the ring, shortly following by Peking Tom who received the same.

The fight was long, violent and bloody. Everything I feared it would be. The one saving grace being I was enough rows back not to be on the receiving end of any blood and saliva flying out of the men's mouths. I fail to see how this is entertainment, but it clearly serves some purpose for those who watch it. If it were not for the cheering of the crowd, howling with an almost bestial excitement, the fight itself would have seemed rather tragic. However, I am learning fast, that judging how anyone is adapting to and surviving the new state of affairs is not a useful task. After what must have been an hour and a half, Tom Tiddler is successful in knocking out his opponent. A dozen workers quickly run into the ring with towels and the victor, raising his hands to the heavens, gives a primal scream that I won't soon forget, met only by the uncontrollable noise of the applauding crowd.

Tom, drenched in sweat and blood, is handed a bottle of vodka which is half consumed and the rest he sprays out onto his admirers. As he is lead out of the ring, he looks at me, but it seems he is looking through me. The victor gives a teeth-filled smile to his fans, which combined with his blood covered face and twirling moustache, gives him the brief flash of a lunatic. It is clear in Tom's eyes though, this is something he loves, this is who he is, and if I do not appreciate it, there seems to be plenty of paying customers who do.

I eventually fight my way out of the crowd to the exit, where punters rifle through mementoes of the day. I purchase a picture of Tom the Hercules and end up with several crudely drawn leaflets in my hand for other events such as dog fights, cock fights and other boxing matches and I remain uncertain in my mind as to how I feel about any of it. The man has undoubtedly made a success of himself, and risen from rejection in the only way he knows.

I cannot stop from crowd-watching at a nearby pub frequented by veterans after the event. The faint muffle of the am dram *Tristan Und Isolde* can be heard coming from the Empire Theatre. As I finish my gin and tonic, my eye is drawn to a tattered poster with an old military mantra gazing over a table of morose down-and-out former soldiers, 'Improvise, Adapt and Overcome'.

Richard Denham

**VOLUNTEERS NEEDED!**

**PAID WORK!**

**WORK FOR THE 'TALLY HO!' CLUB!**

**APPLY AT WADDESDON MANOR NOW!**

# THE HUNTSMAN

**Name: Winston Bath**
**Location: Waddedson Manor, Aylesbury**
**Occupation: Master of Foxhounds**
**Threat level: 1**
**Article clearance: Silver**
**Case file: 09/0745/GBL**

My regular readers will know that I have no views on fox-hunting, either for or against. It may be true that, in the words of Oscar Wilde, it is the unspeakable in pursuit of the uneatable or it may be that it is a necessary part of the countryside that we would be unwise to dispense with when all the usual bastions of society are falling around our ears. Whichever it may be, my visit to the kennels of the Tally Ho! Club was an eye-opener, as this interview will reveal.

**Thank you for agreeing to meet me Mr. Bath.**

By Jove, they've sent a bloody woman! Oh well, tally ho and all that, what? Can you hear me over the noise of these blasted foxhounds? Damned hounds.

**Are you about to go on a hunt?**

Yes, bad timing on your part I'm afraid, old girl. You can come with if you like, I'll make an exception to the rules if it's useful to your Ministry friends.

**Well I can ride but –**

No, no, say no more. My pleasure. Whip! Boy! Jodhpurs, hat, gloves, crop for the lady please.

**There is quite a gathering of people by your tent, I notice, Mr Bath.**

Yes, they are our guest riders from the city, come up for a day's sport. They're not regulars you see, but well, they pay their cap and they are all gentleman. A lovely day like this, a bit of English air, bloody lovely, what? The ladies, they won't be coming, so I hope the Ministry realises I really am going against the grain letting you ride with us.

**Well I don't actually –**

No, no, say no more old girl. It's a brave new world, and a queer one at that. The ladies will be taking afternoon tea while the gents are away so you really are privileged.

**How has business been for you since the war?**

Blooming, old girl, blooming. You see, it's a damned old state Blighty is in, isn't it. People need to escape for a day, let off some steam, enjoy a good old ride and a day's hunt before they go back to whatever misery awaits them. We're never short of quarry for them either; would you like to meet their quarry today.

**Meet? The fox? Are they tame, then?**

Why not, what? Whip! Whip! Open the kennel door, boy. Our guest from the Ministry wants to meet our quarry. **At this point I should tell the readers that, inside a cramped and filthy shed, was a man, little more than a boy, really, who stood up and looked apprehensively at my host and me.**

There you go, old boy, what was your name again?
'Wilfrid, sir.'

Ah that's the one; this man here is Wilfrid, good sport he is too. I hope you've eaten well, you'll need your strength what?

'Oh yes sir, I've eaten like a king, not too much I hope, perish the thought.'

That's the spirit!

**Wilfrid is the quarry?**

Oh yes, friendly enough fellow too. A volunteer, actually. You see, normally we'd pay the magistrates a sum for the villains, rogues and nancies they'd dealt with, but well, bit of a shortage of criminals at the moment I'm afraid, what with the courts not being what they used to be. Every now and then a bobby will bring us a blaggard off their own steam but well, volunteers are as good as any, and they're not so mean spirited either!

**Wilfrid, why have you volunteered for this? Do you know what's going to happen?**

Oh yes m'lady. The family are in a bad way at the moment, and what with father's injury, we're nigh on destitute. I got given this here pamphlet at the market, volunteers wanted; it pays handsome, it does. Anyone who escapes the hunt is paid very handsome indeed. I'd be able to keep my family fed for a year I reckon. It's not ideal m'lady, but work is work isn't it and I'm grateful for it. These gentlemen could spend their time with villains but they've given us honest folk a chance to benefit to. And I hear a good number of people escape the hunt don't they Mr. Bath?

'Well, yes, yes, of course. Wouldn't be sport if we won every time would it?'

All I need to do is get away, and if I do, the next day I'll be paid.

'Well, we're almost ready old boy, get yourself dressed and the boy will collect you in a few moments.'

**After a few minutes, Wilfrid is led out in new clothes and he is given a moment to address the crowd. He seems overwhelmed to be given the honour and I found it hard not to rush the platform and carry him off. But, as we all know, the strength is always with the numbers and I daresay that it will surprise none of my regular readers when I say that I was in little doubt that they would have been as happy with two to chase as with one. After Wilfrid's heartfelt hope that he would give them good sport, the platform was handed over to Winston Bath, a man who I hope rots in Hell [Legal – check that for me will you, like a darling?]**

Ladies and gentleman, our guest of honour for the day, Wilfrid Seymour. A local fellow from the village, who has kindly volunteered to be our quarry for the day. He has signed all the necessary paperwork and is ready for a good day's sport. Just remember ladies and gentleman, Wilfrid is an honest sort and is no villain, so Queensbury rules apply, that goes to you especially Sir Granston. However, sport is sport, and no quarter will be given should the foxhounds win the day.

**Mr Bath, I ... I would prefer not to ride, I don't feel too well.**

Oh blast, suit yourself. I suppose it's good for the tradition of the thing, but do let the Ministry know I offered you to ride and they are always welcome here if they wish to join in the fun.   Ok chaps, all ready? Tally ho!

**It was a while before the horses returned and by then the small talk of the Club's ladies had worn me almost to the point of screaming. In fact, screaming was very much in my mind when I saw**

**the bloodied muzzles of the hounds and the tattered thing which had once been Wilfrid Seymour being dragged behind Bath's horse. As a journalist, I should have asked more questions, but I couldn't bring myself to speak to the animal. This didn't stop him filling us in on what happened. Apparently, according to the ladies, when there is no fee payable – in other words, every time – they have a whip-round for the family. Whip-round is not the word I would use. Whipping would be more appropriate.**

And there we have it; poor fellow didn't get too far once the hounds caught up with him. What an awfully good sport though. Ladies and gentleman, if you would like to retire and the evening's entertainments will commence at seven o' clock. Boy, bury Mr. Seymour will you, thank you. Now, Miss … er … the ladies will have some evening attire if you wish to join us for tonight's pleasantries. I say, whatever happened to Miss … er?

**But he was talking to my back – I needed to leave as I have never needed to leave anywhere before. In a final note to my readers, if ever I disappear, along with others already noted, please check the trophy room of the Tally Ho! Club – I noticed some of them eyeing my ponytail with some interest.**

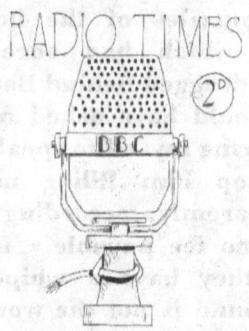

## Whitehall Radio – 600kHz MW

Peter Dawson - God Save The King

Anne Shelton - A Nightingale Sang In
Berkeley Square

MESSAGE FROM THE XXII COMMITTEE (REF:
Rationing)

Vera Lynn - There'll Always Be An England

Anne Shelton - Coming In On A Wing And A
Prayer

MESSAGE FROM THE XXII COMMITTEE (REF:
Earl Wathmere)

Vera Lynn - Now Is The Hour

MESSAGE FROM THE XXII COMMITTEE (REF:
English Resistance atrocities)

MESSAGE FROM THE XXII COMMITTEE (REF:
Occupied Zone)

MESSAGE FROM THE XXII COMMITTEE (REF: Bristol)

MESSAGE FROM THE XXII COMMITTEE (REF: His Majesty)

Albert Farrington - Rule, Britannia

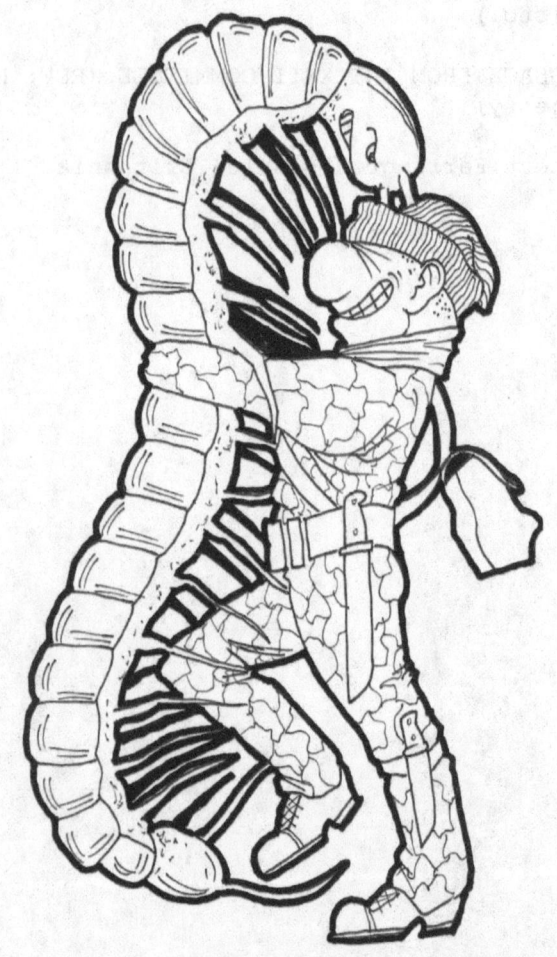

'*Even the creepy-crawlies don't like the Roundheads!*'
- Southern Herald

# THE PARTISAN

**Name: 'Fairfax IV'**
**Location: Unknown**
**Occupation: Criminal/traitor**
**Threat level: 5**
**Article clearance: Silver (amendment 1.3 and 8.3**
**applies)**
**Case file: [omitted]**

**Unusually, I am unable to write any preamble to this interview, as it will put my interviewee in danger. I will refer to him as 'Fairfax' but in fact 'he' could easily be a 'she', so my regular readers must take no detail in the following pages as gospel. It might be true. It might not. Who knows?**

**Fairfax, for my report we are inside a pigeon coop, what is this for?**

Messages, quite impressive isn't it? Who would have thought that the Resistance were such pigeon fanciers? Oh, please ignore my man who has had a Thompson pointed at you the entire time, and I am sorry for the blindfolded journey from our collection point, but, you can't be too careful. Allow me to see your papers if you'd be so kind.

**Your man, over there, why is he laughing at my papers?**

Ah, that is 'Waller', he's French-Canadian, so forgive him; he means no disrespect. He finds your name amusing. Marriane, as I am sure you know, is the French symbol of liberty, our Britannia. Come, let us go somewhere a bit quieter, I cannot think over the sound of cooing.

**Are you not fearful of meeting with an employee of the Ministry?**

No, we've taken all necessary precautions. You don't know me, you don't even know if I am in fact Fairfax, or even if I'm with the Resistance necessarily. You don't know if any of what I'm going to tell you is true. You don't know if what I'm going to tell you is simply what I want the Ministry to hear, or whether I have men in the Ministry, or if in fact I'm a Ministry man myself. Truth is real, how we interpret truth, well … It's all a matter of faith, and what we want to believe isn't it?

**Could you explain the name and symbols behind the Resistance? Is it not distracting to your cause?**

Yes, I understand what you mean, but theatricality is all part of it isn't it? I'm more of a realist myself, but the troops love it and it is harmless, and it does the job, so I am happy with that. It's not as clever as we like to think though, quite simple really. The Resistance is nicknamed The Roundheads after those who fought against the Monarchy in the English Civil War. The groups are named after the five men who the King tried to arrest in parliament, and our codenames are all after key figures of the Roundhead movement. Cromwell wanted to be called 'The Lions of Albion', but that was a bit too pompous for the men, so Roundheads stuck. You'll see that I'm Fairfax the fourth, the three before me, well, they're dead now.

I admire the imaginations of some of our men, though; they'd be illustrators or working at the West End if things were different no doubt. The graffiti always makes me smile, I expect you've seen some of our work. There are four main ones that mark the resistance.

Firstly, there is the stencil of the Bulldog. Secondly, there is the cartoon handlebar moustache, I had to have that one explained to me, I think it's to do with keeping a stiff upper lip. Thirdly there is the crossed out silhouette of a man in a bowler hat, a reference to the Ministry and lastly there is Mr. Chad, the cheeky fellow who pops over walls with messages like 'Wot? No Survivors?' and 'Wot? No Enemy?'.

**Why would you condemn the Ministry when they were able to achieve a favourable peace deal?**

That's the thing isn't it? It just doesn't make sense. As you can see from this map, Jerry landed here on the south-coast, the Blitzkrieg moved up to Gloucester in the West and Maldon in the East and London was surrounded, making it as far as Redhill. And then? No surrender, but a cease-fire? The withdrawal of all Axis forces to south of the River Thames and East of the River Exe. Why would Jerry agree to that? Surely the Government couldn't have held out for much longer. Why would Jerry capitulate when total victory was almost at hand?

This is pure speculation, the Ministry is wrapped up in so many layers of lies I doubt they even know what's true anymore but the facts are there, a change of leadership, the effective dissolution of parliament to be replaced with the XXII committee, the arrests – those damned arrests by the Gestapo of men far beyond the occupied zone, the formation of the Ministry, the sudden end to hostilities. My opinion, and I speak for myself here, not the Resistance, is that the Ministry are secret collaborators at best, a puppet government at worst. Yes, they give it all the patriotic bumph, how they negotiated peace at the brink of calamity, the 'victory' of the Nazi withdrawal to the Thames but there are simply too many questions. The Royal Navy, the sheer scale of fighting men still at their disposal, the Empire for God's sake, Canada, India, Australia.

**Do you have contacts overseas?**

The naval blockade is extremely effective; I'll say no more than that.

151

## What activities does the Resistance undertake?

Oh you know I can't answer that, let's just say anything that hinders the enemy. A lot of it is peaceful, a war of words and ideas. Some of it, I'm not particularly proud of, a few occasions I will confess I've been outright ashamed by our actions, but this is war, Queensbury rules rarely apply now.

## The Roundheads are portrayed as violent, lawless bandits and thugs, pretending to be a force for good, who are in love with their own image by the media, did you know that?

Yes of course, and it's to be expected. It doesn't pain me what they write, not at all, but it pains me to know that good people will believe it, such is the power of the written word. Take the Bible for example, Western Civilization developed on a few hundred pages written down two thousand years or so ago. The nonsense they come out with though, half-truths and outright lies, it would be wrong to delude ourselves there is anything independent or there are no vested interests in the media.

I remember when Cromwell II was killed in an ambush that went wrong, we must have had a traitor because it shouldn't have gone the way it did. He put up a brave fight but was peppered with machine gun bullets while trying to escape on a motorcycle, I was lucky enough to get away that day. The media reported it with banner headlines; 'A DAY FOR JUSTICE! The odious and vile criminal William Pepperinge, who was the cruel leader of the anarchist gang, the Roundheads, has taken his own life in shame as being part of the group. The villain, no longer able to live with his great dishonour, crimes and treasonous acts, did approach Government forces and begged their forgiveness before shooting himself in the head with a revolver. The coward may have escaped justice in life but he was posthumously charged with high treason and recognised in court as a traitor, coward and rogue. Fanatical elements of his gang responded by setting fire to a school and a church. The Lord Chief Justice of England and Wales commented 'It is a small mercy that Mr Pepperinge, moved to pitiful child-like sobbing, begged forgiveness for his crimes on his last day, admitting he had mental illness and blaming his wickedness on his atheist upbringing, deviant sexual desires and socialist parents. May God have mercy on his soul. The news of the traitor's death was met with ecstatic applause from gathered crowds outside the court' and so on, and so on. What an absolute nonsense, but I bet there is a part of you that believes some of it, if not all. 'No smoke without fire' eh?

Do you know something, quite interesting really? They call us terrorists, a French word, and do you know to what it originally meant? Abuses of power and horror committed by the state. Now the word has been hijacked by the same people it vilified.

**Did you see this news article? I'll read it in full, if I may.**

**'On 9 June the English resistance stormed the town of Crowborough. The bodies of at least thirty soldiers of the local Home Guard unit were found outside All Saints Church, which was being used as their headquarters, horribly mutilated and terribly mauled. According to the eye-witness accounts of residents of Crowborough, the volunteer soldiers had surrendered to the Roundheads after a brief fire-fight. They came out of the building with a white flag, unarmed and with their hands in the air, at which point they were peppered with machine gun fire.**

**A nearby resident, who has asked to remain anonymous, reported that the English resistance then used a lorry to run over the pile of men, many**

still alive at this point and could hear the hideous cracking of bones and cries of men being crushed to death.

Even more horrifically, the bodies of the thirty men had had their genitals severed, and then placed in their own mouths. The Roundheads then drove off at speed, making sure that each vehicle had the body of a soldier roped to the back of the vehicle which was dragged along the streets and then removed at the edge of town.'
A service will be held for the men who...' and it goes on from there.

And what makes you think that one is any more believable?

**Because I wrote it...**

Well ... I don't know anything about that. I knew about the raid on Crowborough, I have never heard of those accounts before though. Did you see this massacre yourself?

**No but I spoke to the residents who did.**

I'd be curious to know the truth of it.

**Does it not concern you that you are viewed as a criminal and a villain?**

Most heroes are viewed as villains by their peers, most villains viewed as heroes too. It is one of history's cruellest tricks.

**Why do you exist if there is now peace?**

Do you want to know the truth of the matter? I do not think you'll ever believe me but I will tell you anyway. There are no Germans here, not one, not soldiers anyway.

There is simply no occupation. You find that hard to believe don't you but I give you my word. Yes, there is the British Free Corps I suppose, but they are a token gesture, guarding pointless posts in the middle of nowhere, but there is no clear overarching aim. People want to believe the British Army are still fighting heroically, somewhere, but they're not, not to my knowledge.

No, the enemy are not goose-stepping down our streets, there are no swastikas flying from town halls. This, this is why we are branded traitors and criminals. The enemy, the enemy are among us, they are the Ministry.

**That's quite a paranoid claim if you don't mind me saying.**

You're not alone. That's why we have so little support from the people, they don't understand who we are fighting or why. If you allow me to indulge my conspiracy, my paranoia as you put it, I don't think people understand how crippling the terms of the peace were, and what peace? The country is blockaded! The country is tearing itself up from the inside, I would even say that the Ministry are deliberately making things worse. This bizarre state of affairs could surely only exist if the Ministry were on board with it all.

**Do you worry you fight for a world that doesn't want or need to be saved? Do you worry you fight for a world that doesn't exist.**

Excellent question, it exists as long as people are fighting for it.

**Why did you agree to meet me, if you know I am an employee of the Ministry?**

Because we need to believe, I need to believe, that things aren't as hopeless as they seem. I don't know who will read your report, but it is important we have our say. I don't honestly know how long the fires of resistance will burn or what will happen to the Roundheads but I honestly believe we speak for truth, justice, honour and reason. It is fragile though, as in any Empire built on hope and ideals. It would only take one big mistake, and the whole Resistance could come crumbling down. I won't delude myself we are going to convert thousands to our ranks, but we are asking questions that need to be answered. And let me ask you, please; Would you still fight on for a cause you believed in even if you knew it was hopeless? If you know you were fighting a battle that few now cared about or understood? Would you endure, even if it cost you your life? What is it Maryanne, that you believe? I expect no one at the Ministry has asked you that before.

**Thank you for speaking to me, Fairfax.**

Before you go there are two things. First of all, for security, I will ask that you stay here for two nights before you go. It will allow our group to move on so that you cannot report back on our position. You will be guarded and well cared for I promise, but you can never be too sure. Secondly I'd ask, that for just ten minutes, you put down your pen and notepad and allow me to show you something, something that may change your mind about, well, about everything. In the words of Oliver Cromwell, 'I beseech you in the bowels of Christ think it possible you may be mistaken.'

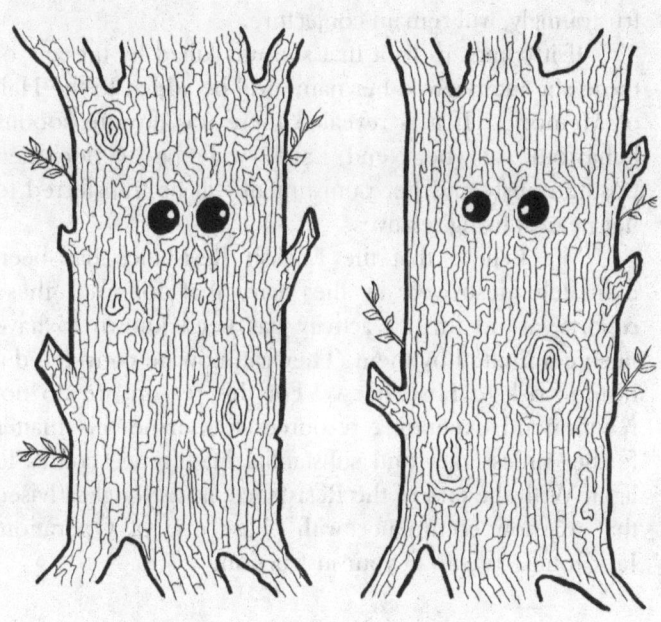

*'No Cromwell, I've got nothing to hide either'*
- Southern Herald

Dear Sirs,

The above was the last report we received from Maryanne Coleman. What happened to her after this is unknown. We did in fact receive all her interviews, hand delivered to the front desk of The Ministry, but whether this was with her consent and the identity of who delivered them, frustratingly, will remain conjecture.

If it comes to light that she was killed by the any of those she interviewed her name will be added to the Hall of Memories. If it is revealed there was any treasonous behaviour at her end, she will be condemned posthumously and her punishment will be transferred to her nearest living relatives.

We believe that the English Resistance has been ultimately destroyed in the years that followed these reports, as no further activity has been known to have been committed by them. They can now be considered a historic risk to His Majesty. For this reason, we do not recommend expending resources to pursue this matter further unless new and substantial intelligence comes to light. With the end of the Resistance, it is strongly advised that we now commence with phase one of Operation: Jack Jones. We await your instruction.

Yours faithfully,

Agent Steed - 2565

-.-. .- -. -.. .. .. .- -. / ...
.... .. .-- . ... / ... . . -. / ..
-. / - .... . / .. .-. .. ... ....
/ ... . .- --.-- / .-- .... . - -
/ .- .-. . / -.-- --- .. .-. / --
- .-. -. . .- . ... ..-.. / -.. -
-- / .-- --- .. / .-- .-. . - /
..- ... / - --- / -.-. --- -- .
-. -.- . / ..- .. -. .. -. -. --.
..-..

**Citizen Survivor's Handbook**
**By Richard Denham & Steve Hart**

**The prepper's guide with a difference. Includes a foreword by TV star and best-selling author Cody Lundin.**

During the 1940's Britain suffered a national catastrophe that would become known as 'The Great Tribulation' by its survivors. The remnant of His Majesty's Government formed a department known as The Ministry of Survivors, the mandate of this office being to help, guide and inform the public through the anarchy around them. During the early years they produced and issued a handbook known as 'The Citizen Survivor's Guidebook'.

    However, as the situation became more desperate, the guidance within this book quickly became redundant. The Ministry deemed that the only remaining course of action was to produce a second edition; informing people to evacuate the chaos of the towns and cities and flee to the countryside, focusing on wilderness survival and how to be self-sufficient on the move. This is a surviving copy of that handbook.

www.blkdogpublishing.com